SKI THE MOUNTAIN

Ski the Mountain

Helen Markley Miller

Illustrated by Nancy Grossman

DOUBLEDAY & COMPANY, INC.

GARDEN CITY, NEW YORK 1965

SKI THE MOUNTAIN

I

*F*irst snow fell on an October night that had begun with wind and rain. But toward dawn a low half-moon sliced in and out of scudding clouds to hide and then reveal the fanglike peaks of Idaho's Sawtooth Range sweeping endlessly north and endlessly south above a long, snow-whitened valley. Near the foothills of the lesser mountains facing the range the clustered log buildings of a ranch were mere specks of black on white in a still world of space and height.

The ranch world did not remain silent. Down from the gulch beyond the barn a dark shadow lumbered on four huge feet to pad around the outside of the corral. The horses penned inside the massive pole fence neighed in wild alarm and began circling the enclosure on pounding hoofs. Under the lean-to on the corral side of the barn two milch cows scrambled to their feet and bawled a warning to their calves in a nearby pen. The calves answered plaintively, sheep bleated in panic, and a shepherd dog leaped from his gunny-sack bed under the cabin doorstep and ran yelping toward the corral. Stopping suddenly, he sniffed the air, growled deep in his throat, bristled, and then retreated toward the cabin door, the increased frenzy of his howls begging for human help against danger.

Gordon Stevens stirred restlessly under the patchwork comforters on his bed in the loft, but as the barnyard sounds and the dog's continued barking pricked through heavy sleep, he roused slowly to complete wakefulness.

"Something after the calves," he muttered and swung his legs over the edge of the bed to slide his feet into his boots.

Hastily pulling on his jeans, he scrambled down the ladder to meet his mother as she hurried from the bedroom. The kerosene lamp that she held spread a dim yellow glow over the log walls and ceiling beams of the big room that served as kitchen, dining, and living quarters.

"What is it, Gordy?" she asked, her voice sounding tight and sharp. "What's out there?"

"Coyote, probably. Only it's a lot of fuss for just an old coyote slinking around. Maybe it's that bear—the one that got a calf up on the range last week. I'd better go see."

Reaching for the rifle that stood in the corner of the room, he threw the lever to see that the cartridge was in place, but his mother moved closer, placing fingers that trembled on his arm. The lamp shook in her other hand, and in its tremulous light he saw that her eyes were wide with fear.

"No, Gordy. You can't go out there. Not in the dark this way. If it's a bear—"

"But I have to, Mother. The calves—"

"I'd rather the thing would take every one of the calves than have you—hurt."

Gordon glanced at his mother in love and understanding. She looked like a frightened girl, with the fringe of brown hair all tumbled over her forehead and her braids roughened from sleeping. She hadn't been like this, scared of everything, when they had first come to the ranch, early in the summer of 1900, but ever since his father had been killed last winter, buried under those tons of ice and rock that had roared down the gulch, she had been nervous and afraid. The fear was not for herself, Gordon knew, but that some danger might take away her son too, that harm might come to his twin sister, Molly.

"Wait until morning," his mother urged. "I've heard dreadful tales about the bears in these mountains. A bear can—kill."

His mind began to see the pictures that were in her thoughts, pictures of bared fangs and great slashing claws. After all, maybe he wasn't so eager to rush out there and tangle with any old bear. He patted her hand and broke away from her to cross to the door, open it, and look out on moonlight slanting across thin new snow. The dog Pete jumped up on his master, barked frantically, and then ran a little way toward the corral and back as if urging the destruction of danger. The cows and horses were still keeping up their noise, and the hens joined in now with shrill squawking.

"If it's a bear, it's still around," Gordon said. "Look, Mother, I ought to go after it."

"No. We'll ask Lars to get it for us. In the morning."

Gordon hesitated. Lars Antonsson was a good trapper and an obliging neighbor who would track and shoot the bear and think the hunting fun. But it might take two or three days, and a bear fattening for its winter hibernation could do much damage to the range calves in that time. Gordon thought of the huge imprints he had seen on the soft ground near the spring up on the range, of the torn carcass he had found in a clump of aspen. A bear's claws could slash a boy to death as easily as they had the calf. He shuddered a little and gave into his mother's wishes all at once, but he felt ashamed to realize that his yielding brought him utter relief.

"All right," he said. "I'll wait until morning, and we'll get Lars to help. Pete's likely scared the bear off anyway with all that barking. Maybe the sound of a gun will send the thing away for the rest of the night." He shot the rifle from the door a couple of times and then, whistling to Pete, collared the dog and pulled it inside. "Don't want to lose old Pete," he muttered. "He might get up enough spunk to follow and tie into that bear."

Molly, awakened by the shots, came pattering from the bedroom in her bare feet, her long pink nightgown held from the floor, her straw-colored pigtails standing out from her head, her eyes bright with excitement. She always came out of the sleep fog the instant she opened those blue eyes of hers because she was afraid she might miss something, Gordon thought, a little enviously. Even if they were twins, they weren't much alike. She was quick and impulsive and daring, while he was slower to act, slower to reach decision. Sometimes he almost felt as if Molly were his younger sister instead of his twin, perhaps because she was always bubbly with enthusiasm. Every commonplace happening on the ranch was a lively adventure to her: the birth of a new colt, the first hardy spring flowers, even the white curtain of a blizzard driving down from the mountains.

"What's wrong, Gordy?" she asked eagerly. "I heard shooting. Is there a coyote around? Or a weasel in the henhouse? Did you get it?"

"It's a bear, I guess," he answered shortly. "The shots were to scare it off."

"A bear! Oh, Gordy! Maybe it didn't scare. You're going out after it, aren't you? Hurry. Before it hurts anything."

"In the morning," his mother answered for him. "When it's light."

"Oh, no, Mother. No, Gordy. Now. Right now, before it gets away. What if it takes a slash at one of the horses? Or gets a calf? Hurry, Gordy. Father would have been out there fast."

"Gordon's not your father, Molly," her mother said in sharp reproof. "After all, Gordy is only fourteen. Too young to—"

"Almost fifteen we are, Mother," Molly persisted. "That's old enough to do what has to be done."

"Go back to bed, Molly," her mother ordered firmly. "Gordy isn't going out there. The bear's likely gone off anyway. The animals have quieted. Both of you go back to bed. I think I'll stay up. It's after four now, and I'll not sleep again. I'll call you when breakfast is ready."

Molly did not say anything more, only put all that she was thinking into one disappointed look at her brother. Dropping the folds of her gown to the floor, she turned on bare feet and swept into the bedroom, trailing pink behind her with the dignity of a princess in one of those books she was always reading. Gordon had to grin because pink flannel and bare feet and tangled yellow pigtails didn't exactly go with queenly displeasure, but he knew well enough what she meant to convey by walk and look: her knight, whom she loved and trusted, had failed in the quest.

Let her be disgusted with me, he told himself as he climbed to his loft. I'm no knight out of *Ivanhoe* or any of those old King Arthur stories. I'm just a boy trying to ride in his father's stirrups and finding them set a lot too long.

The cold bed warmed slowly, but Gordon couldn't go back to sleep because he kept thinking with hurting loneliness of the father he had lost. "Big Jim," the valley people called Jim Stevens, and now when they talked of him, they always said, "Big Jim was a good man." By "good" they meant strong and fair-dealing and courageous—a man powerful enough to tackle the problems of a tough and cruel country. No boy ever could fill the place of Big Jim, Gordon thought.

Behind closed eyes memories came. When the news of the snowslide had reached him last February, he'd been at school in Hailey, a town on the other side of the mountain, for the valley had no school. Although his parents had allowed him to remain at home during that first difficult year on the ranch, they were unwilling to allow him to miss more of his education, even if it meant a first separation for him and Molly—a separation necessary because there wasn't enough money to send both of them. He was just beginning to adjust to being away from home when the news came. Mose Field, at whose house he boarded, came into the schoolroom and took him outside to tell him about Father, and in that moment of the telling the world had seemed to tilt out of place. Mose knew what to say to bring him back to reality.

"You'll have to get to the ranch somehow," he said. "Your ma and Molly can't live there without a man. But God knows how you'll make it with the pass buried under fourteen feet of snow."

"How did the man with the message get here?" Gordon asked.

"Came around south by the desert road."

"Then that's the way I'll have to go home."

Gordon made it to the ranch, although he was almost two weeks on the way. There were days and miles of tramping the desert road that circled the mountains to enter through a canyon at the far northern end of the valley. The few ranchers along the way were kind about giving him meals and beds, sometimes there were rides, but when he reached the head of the valley, there was still its long white floor stretching away to the southwest under the tremendous toothed peaks. He borrowed a pair of skis from old Smiley Tufts, the storekeeper in the settlement there, and trudged the last miles to the ranch. He wasn't any good on skis, and the snows seemed to have a stubborn life of their own, bent on holding him back. When he stumbled to the ranch door late at night, his mother cried over him, but Molly said, "Pfoo, what's all the fuss about? I knew you'd come, Gordy."

The next morning he'd begun his job of trying to be man enough to do his father's work, and he hadn't been ready. Wasn't ready even now, he told himself. Not going out to shoot that bear was sure proof that he wasn't. He hadn't needed Molly's words or look to tell him what he should do; he had known well enough. Then why had he stayed safely in the cabin?

"You were scared," he whispered to himself in harsh honesty. "That's what you were. You thought of what a bear might do to you, and you didn't want to chance it."

And so he had let the bear get away to kill more of the range calves, although he knew that they couldn't afford to lose even one more calf. He'd have to do better than that if he meant to run the ranch the way his father had.

Gordon didn't like the blunt truths that his inner self was telling him, and he tried to put them out of his mind and go back to sleep. But it wasn't any good, and after a time he jumped out of bed and pulled on his clothes to climb down the ladder toward the good smell of frying bacon and the muffled thud of a spoon against the side of the pancake bowl. A stack or two of his mother's flapjacks, and he might still be able to face knowing that he'd have to help Lars track and shoot the bear.

The kitchen was full of the lamp's yellow glow, for the light was still dim outside. Gordon smiled at his mother, who was turning thick slices of sizzling bacon at the hot range, and then, crossing to the western window, he looked across the valley to the great peaks standing ghostly in the steel-gray dawn. A morning habit, almost a ritual, was this inspection, for the day's weather was made in the mountains, and weather ruled the lives of all who lived in the valley.

"Going to be sunny," he told his mother as he turned to wash at the bench near the door. "That skiff of snow we had last night will melt before noon."

She spooned pancakes onto the smoking griddle, where they sizzled in the fat and made a blue smoke. When he moved back to the window, she came to look over his shoulder.

"Yes," she said, "the snow will go down here in the valley, but there's staying snow low on the peaks. Winter began up there last night."

She sighed as she turned back to the stove to watch the pancakes. He knew why she sighed. When they had first come to the valley, she had liked to watch the changing glory of the great peaks; now, since the mountains had taken Jim Stevens, she seldom glanced at them, and when she did, it was with a distrust that was close to fear. Gordon watched the rugged summits sharpen their outlines in the growing light and knew that he too dreaded the snows and almost hated the mountains.

"I wish," he said bitterly, "that Father had never found this valley on that prospecting trip of his. I wish he'd never taken out a claim on this half section of sagebrush and forest. I wish he'd never brought us here from Ohio. And more than anything, I wish we weren't saddled with this blamed cattle ranch."

"You know he had a plan, Gordy. A big place, slowly and soundly built through the years, large enough to bring security for us all. He always said that here you and Molly would grow strong in body and spirit. The ranch was a good dream—while he was alive. Now—"

"Now it's just a nightmare—the kind you can't shake off. And those old mountains are part of it. They—they just sit on your chest and grin."

Jean Stevens smiled a little as she slid the steaming hotcakes to a plate and carried them to the table in the living end of the big room. "Come on, Gordy. Eat your cakes while they're hot. Molly will be in right away." As he obeyed, she went on, "It's a good thing one of us likes the ranch."

"Oh, Molly!" Gordon muttered impatiently. "She loves every cow and calf, every dry old twig of sagebrush. She even likes the mountains and the snow. Where is she anyway?"

"Down at the barn hunting for bear tracks."

"She would be—before it's even sunrise."

Molly never could wait to plunge into any excitement that the ranch offered. Funny, he thought, she looked just like her mother but had her father's gay and courageous spirit. And he looked like his father, the same sandy hair, gray eyes, and broad shoulders; yet he seemed to have all his mother's fears. Like her, he could find no joy in this fight to win over mountains and weather and bears that came in the night to steal from the herds.

"If we could only sell the place!" he said, buttering his cakes mechanically and pouring syrup over them.

"We can't, Gordy. Who would want this lonely spot so far from any town?"

"Well then, if we could just get money enough somehow to move back to the East!"

"We can't. You know we have exactly eight dollars and sixty-three cents. Even after we sold the steers this last fall, even before we stocked up on winter food, goodness knows there wasn't enough for a move and a start in a new place."

"No sale, no money," he said ruefully. "No money, stuck here."

"There'll be money someday, if we can build up the herd," his mother reminded him.

Build up the herd, he thought. The only way to get money enough ahead to leave the ranch. And he had let that bear go roaming off to steal more of the heifers that would increase the herd.

The door banged open and Molly bounced into the room, her cheeks reddened by the chill air, wet snow clinging to her boots and the cuffs of her jeans. Slipping off her leather jacket, she tossed it carelessly in the direction of a chair.

"It *was* a bear!" she announced, her clear voice high and excited. "A great big one. He didn't get in, but he left huge old paw prints in the snow all around the corral, and there's one place where he stood on his hind feet and looked over. Glory, I wish I'd seen him. Why didn't you go shoot him, Gordy, when you had a good chance? Why didn't you?"

Before he could answer, his mother intervened. "Never mind, Molly. Hang up your coat and then wash and come eat your breakfast. As soon as you've finished, you may saddle Phoebe and ride for Lars. He'll get the bear for us."

Molly dipped her fingertips in water, dried them on the towel, and then slid into place at the table to eat in silence, but Gordon caught her glancing accusingly at him over the edge of her glass of milk as she drank.

"I'm all through, Mother," she said breathlessly. "I'll go for Lars now. Can I go with him when he hunts the bear? I've never seen a really big one. Is it a grizzly, do you suppose, Gordy?"

"No. There aren't any grizzlies left around here. It's a

black bear, likely. And Lars isn't going to want a girl along
when he hunts it. Your job is to bring Lars back here as
fast as you can. Tracking ought to be easy for him in this
new snow."

"For him? Aren't you going along?"

"Haven't decided," Gordon answered, his tone a little
sharp because he couldn't stand the look in her eyes that
said that her faith in him was even in the least shaky. She
was a little more than his sister; she was his twin, the other
half of him in a way, and he wanted her to keep on thinking

he was everything brave and fine. "Hurry and get ready," he said gruffly. "I'll saddle Phoebe for you before I milk."

Lifting the milk pails from their rack by the door, he walked to the barn, Pete cavorting beside him. The valley lay gray and cold in the shadow of the eastern hills, but the sun was brushing a long shaft of rosy light across the tips of highest peaks in the range. Bristling and whining, Pete sniffed at the prints the bear had left around the corral, and Gordon saw that the tracks angled off behind the barn toward the opening of the gulch leading up to the high mesa and the hills beyond where the herd ranged. He caught and saddled Molly's horse, Phoebe, and brought it up to her as she came from the cabin.

"Ride fast," he told her, "and get Lars back here before this snow goes."

Molly mounted, not bothering to answer him. Gordon looked after her unhappily as she cantered off across the five miles of sagebrush that stretched between the ranch and Lars Antonsson's cabin, hidden from sight behind a hogback ridge that nosed out from the foothills. She didn't know what hard work it was for a boy to turn man too soon.

II

*L*ars *Antonsson*, their nearest neighbor, had come to the valley from Sweden in 1898, two years before the Stevens family had taken out their land. Educated in his own country, he now spoke English well, although his sentences often were twisted and sounds did not always come right for him. He didn't have much of a ranch— a few acres, a clean one-room cabin, a shed for his one horse, a little patch of meadow for hay.

"All an old trapper have need for," he had told Gordon. "For wife I have the mountains. Always they are changing, minute from minute, like a woman change with mood. For friend I have my skis. It is enough."

Each winter he ran his trapline in the mountains, traveling on skis over the deep snows. Since he was familiar with the habits of all the forest animals, he would know exactly how to track the bear.

Knowing that Molly and Lars could not return for an hour or so, Gordon puttered with the barn chores. He brought out Guinevere's calf and let it work on one side of its mother while he milked the other side of the udder. Then he repeated the process with Rowena and her offspring. He had to smile when he thought of how Molly had named the cows that their father bought for the ranch, always choosing fancy names from some book she was reading. To him Guinevere was Gwen, and Rowena was Weenie. When he finished the milking, he carried the pails to the kitchen lean-to, strained the milk into flat pans for the cream to rise, and took the pails in for his mother to wash. She was mixing bread dough, and the room smelled of spicy cookies already in the oven.

"Pile the woodbox high this morning, Gordy," she said. "Bread baking takes a lot of wood."

After he had carried in big armloads, he filled the water pails from the constantly flowing spigot outside the kitchen door. The buried pipe tapped a spring high in the hills, and the water came down with such force that it seldom froze in the winter. The overflow was ditched off to irrigate the meadows. As he set the pails on the bench, his mother was taking the cookies from the oven.

"I wish you didn't have to work so hard," he grumbled, helping himself from the pan. "Washing, ironing, baking, churning, making candles and soap. You'd think it was 1840 instead of 1902. You have to do as much as those pioneer women did who came West in covered wagons."

"Goodness, Gordy, I don't mind the work," she responded. "Just—other things sometimes."

He went back to the barn hating the ranch more than ever. His mother was not strong, and all the work, even with Molly's help, kept her thinner than she should be. He fed the stock, turned the few sheep out to graze on the nearby hills, mended a broken slat in the chickenpen fence, but all the time he was keeping a watch over the flat for Molly and Lars. He saw them when they rode out from behind the hogback, two specks moving fast over the snowy plain dotted with darker sagebrush. Lars on his big black horse dwarfed Molly on her little mare. Gordon went to open the ranch gate, and Molly galloped through first, laughing as she slipped from the saddle and shouting, "I beat you, Lars, you old slowpoke."

"This little Molly," Lars said, smiling at Gordon as he dismounted slowly, "is always in hurry. Old man of sixty-eight year, he must have time for slow moving."

Gordon grinned as he looked at the short and compact body of his elderly friend and at the ruddy face, cheeks hardened by the mountain winds. The only sign age seemed to have left on Lars was his white hair, worn shaggy in the way of the valley men.

"You may think you're slowing up, Lars," Gordon said admiringly, "but there's nobody around here who can get around as fast as you do on skis."

"For that—what you call getting around—I am giving thanks. But Molly say you have the bear last night. We will get him. He have left prints?"

"A clear track leading off upgulch. But before you go, come on in the house. Mother's baking cookies, and she'll have the coffeepot on for you."

"Jean knows that for coffee I have much liking, or I would not be true Swedish." Lars squinted up at the sun just topping the hills. "The snow will hold long enough for me to drink a warming cup. The bear, he will not run far away."

Over his coffee Lars asked, "You will come with me, Gordon—to shoot the bear?"

"We—ell," Gordon began, trying to think up reasons for not going and coming up lamely with, "there's a lot of work needs doing around here."

His mother broke in quickly. "I'd rather Gordon didn't go. It will be dangerous, Lars—hunting bear?"

Lars looked from mother to son, keen eyes studying them both, but his expression did not change. "Dangerous? Maybe. Like many duties here in mountains." He went on more slowly, evidently thinking out his words. "But man must face danger many times if he is to remain true to— to that something inside which tell him he is a man. I do not say it well."

"You say it just right, Lars," Molly put in, giving her brother another of those questioning, disappointed looks. "And anyway, who's afraid of any old bear with you along? Take me. I want to see the bear. Take me, Lars."

The old man shook his head, although he smiled at Molly's eagerness. "No, Molly. Hunting bear is not for girls. It is for the man of this home to go."

Gordon did not see how he could say out loud that he would much rather stay safely at home. To himself he could admit that he wasn't eager to face a bear, but he could not let his friend know—nor Molly.

"I—I guess I'd better go along," he told his mother and then waited, hoping that she would forbid his going.

Lars, however, did not give her a chance to object again. "He will go, Jean. And I will see that no harm comes to your boy. Your horse is saddled, Gordon?"

Reluctantly, Gordon went to the corral, saddled his horse Lance (named Lancelot by Molly), tied it with the big black, and went back to the cabin. His mother was wrapping a packet of sandwiches for their lunch, her eyes troubled, her lips looking thin and scared.

"I wish you wouldn't go, Gordy," she said. "You must be very careful."

Gravely Lars waited at the open door, not saying anything, only looking determined. Gordon tried to smile reassuringly at his mother, but he knew the smile was not very convincing.

"I'll be all right," he told her, speaking gruffly to cover up what he felt they all must know: that he had no stomach for this hunting. Pete jumped up on him, barking and begging to go along.

Molly collared the dog and smiled up at her brother. "You'll shoot that old bear all by yourself, Gordy," she said. "I know you will."

"That's what you think," he muttered, but as he hurried to join the relentless old trapper, he felt a little better because her faith in him was restored. Molly loved him so much that she could never stay cross with him for long.

Lars took the lead, following the bear's tracks in the snow of the narrow cattle trail leading up to the mesa above. He sat small in his saddle, his short, stocky legs held out stiffly from the sides of his big horse, and as he rode up out of the shadows, the sun glinted on his white hair, making it look to Gordon like a silken ruffle attached to the battered old blue wool cap. At the edge of the mesa top the old man leaned from his saddle to study the bear tracks.

"Pretty big, aren't they?" Gordon asked.

"Yes, big. I think maybe only grizzly could make track like this. Silvertip."

"Grizzly!" Gordon exclaimed, dismayed. "But, Lars, you know there aren't any grizzlies here now."

"Grizzly, he do not come often to these mountains. But he come. Two years ago I shoot fine big one. Then I never see one again. Now I think one is here."

"But, Lars—well, look, grizzlies are fierce. We'd better turn back. I—I think Mother would want us to."

"Yes, that is true about Jean. She would be scared for you."

"Then let's just go back to the house. I guess the thing won't be getting any more calves anyway. It's hibernating time. That old grizzly will be hunting himself a cave soon."

Lars shook his head. "We will go on. We will get the bear."

"But if it's a grizzly—"

"Then it kind of change things, that's all. Grizzly is hard to kill, but there is a way. I will teach you that way, and then you will be ready. Readiness is only way to prepare for danger."

The old trapper touched his horse's side with a heel and rode on. Gordon followed, resentment filling his thoughts. Lars was just a stubborn old Swede—had to do what he set out to do when he must know it would be a lot more sensible to turn back. A grizzly was not an animal with which one fooled. Gordon shivered a little, almost deciding to go home by himself, only—well, then Molly would look at him the way she had last night, and Lars would be disappointed in him. There was nothing to do but ride on across the sloping mesa to the high sharp ridge that sliced down from the higher hills above.

On the crest of the ridge Lars pulled up. Squaring his shoulders into the sage-scented October breeze, he pointed to the valley below, where the ranch buildings had crept into sunshine. Then he waved a hand toward the bulk of the great range, driving its glacier-laden spires into a cloudless sky.

"The mountains," he said quietly, "always they are there. They have strength to give."

Gordon looked down, hating all the beauty of his home valley. He saw the sagebrush plain that stretched a full mile from the ranch house to the two strips of snow-covered meadow, shut in by the line of the road fence. Beyond the fence the road was a glistening, snowy line, scarcely more than a trail, angling to follow the curves of the brawling, new-born Salmon River. On the other side of the stream more sagebrush climbed to meet forested hills that swept westward in blue-gray waves toward the immaculate mountains. The man-made buildings and road, the tiny meadows grubbed from the sagebrush plain seemed puny and power-less under the serene peaks.

"You do not like this wilderness of mountain?" Lars asked, looking keenly at Gordon's resentful face.

"I don't know. I suppose it's all right," Gordon began slowly. He went on then in a rush of words to let out all the thoughts worrying around in his mind. "But, Lars, the mountains shut us in the valley—so far from towns. And I want to go to school. I want to learn. I like books. I like having friends of my own age, and I'm the only boy in this whole blamed valley. Look down there at the road—not a soul in sight. There's our ranch, squatting right in the mid-dle of nothing. Can't see your place for the hogback. Can't see Fred Curley's place. And he hasn't got any kids—just that funny little dried-up wife."

"Fred and Sue have been good to you and your mother."

"Sure. I know. And don't think I don't appreciate all they did last summer to help us run the ranch without Father. But they aren't much company for me."

"The McCartys—you have forgot them. They have sons."

"Sure. Sure. Fifteen miles down the valley, and anyway all three of the McCarty boys are too old to pay any attention to a kid like me. And it's twenty miles to Stanley. Why they bother to give that settlement a name I can't see. There's nothing there but a couple of cabins and a combination store-saloon. No people. Just Smiley Tufts and a couple of old prospectors."

Lars nodded as if he understood and then bent to study the tracks in the snow. "We are forgetting the bear," was all he said.

The prints of the great pads left the ridge here to cut down into a small canyon. The two horses were skittish now, shying at every bush, snorting, trying to turn toward home.

"What's the matter with them?" Gordon asked crossly.

"They smell bear." Lars pointed down into the gully. "He is down there, I think, where it is free of wind, and sun is warm. Bear like to sun themselves. See that clump of willows long way down. We will find him there."

He turned down the steep ridge and Gordon followed sulkily, giving his horse its head, letting it pick a way, for the sunny hillside was honeycombed with gopher holes. It was warm on the canyon floor, and he took off his jacket and tied it behind his saddle.

"Blamed old mountain climate," he muttered crossly. "Freezes you nights, makes you sweat at midday."

Lars was quiet, and when he did speak it was to return to his defense of his valley. "We have one piece of luck anyway, for long time now. We have a road to Outside—short way over the south mountain. Not so when I first came here."

"Road? That cow track? What good is it? Summers it's deep in dust. Takes two days of driving to get over the pass if you've any kind of load. And the other way, down the canyon, it's ninety miles to anything that even looks like a town. Winters there isn't any road, and winter is nine months long. It's like being in prison."

Lars chuckled. "It is true like bears we hibernate, but not bad—when we have plenty food and wood." Checking his horse at the top of a small rise of ground on the canyon floor, he pointed to the clump of willows. "See, our bear have left tracks right to the bushes. He will be in there."

"He'll see us, Lars—or hear us, won't he?" Gordon asked, talking loudly in the hope that the bear would hear and go lumbering off, and Lars would not insist on chasing it.

"No, he is feeding likely. Bears feed head to the wind, and we are right with the wind. So, unless you tell him with your loud talking, he will not know we are here. Listen now and I explain how to shoot grizzly."

"Look, Lars, let's just go home and let the old bear go off in the timber."

"No. We will get him. I will tell you how. To shoot the grizzly is danger unless he is far enough away to fire couple more times before he have reach you. If you wound him and he come at you, then he is nasty. To get him you must put bullet through his heart. Do not aim for head, unless you can hit him in the eye. A bear's skull is sloping. Bullet glance off. Wait until he get close enough to make bullet find heart."

"But, Lars, if he's coming at you—"

"Then keep pumping lead into him as fast as you can."

"Look here, Lars, you talk as if I were going to do the shooting. I don't shoot well enough to—"

"You have hunt the deer with your father."

"Sure. But bear's different. Deer runs away. Bears keeps coming. I'd muff my shot. Maybe wound him but not kill. Then he'd charge us. You do the shooting, Lars."

"It will take both of us, but you will shoot first. It is your bear. He steal your calf, not mine. I will stand by and have the readiness for more shots if they are needed."

"Lars—"

"We will go. We will get the bear. The wind have change. It blow across the canyon now. So. We go over there and come down on him from behind with trees for hiding. Come now."

Wanting nothing so much as to remain safely on Lance's back, Gordon dismounted when Lars did. The skittish horses securely tied in a grove of leafless aspen trees, the two hunters circled high on the side of the hill, stepping carefully through the sagebrush to avoid kicking loose a rock. As they worked down toward the willows, Lars put up a hand to motion for a stop.

"I hear him," he whispered. "He is in there all right."

"Maybe it's just a deer."

"No. Heavy animal—bear. Hear how he break branches when he move."

A loud tearing sound came from the willows. Gordon could not prevent a nervous start, but the trapper only nodded his head in satisfaction.

"He is digging grubs out of rotten logs for food. Soon he have enough. Then he will come out—at this end toward the timber. I will go little way to right. You stay here, and when he come out, shoot. Keep gun ready. Remember, do not shoot until he get close enough to hit."

"Lars," Gordon begged, almost forgetting in his alarm to whisper, "you can't just leave me here alone. I can't shoot a bear. You know I can't."

The old trapper looked at him steadily, the blue eyes hard and bright. "When something have to be done, boy, then you will do it. I know that. It is your bear. First shot is for you. I will not be far—close, so that you can see me. If you miss, I will be ready."

He turned and walked softly across the sunny spot between two clumps of trees. Gordon watched helplessly as the tracks in the melting snow grew between them. Lars took up position behind a pine tree, close enough so that there was at least some comfort from seeing the old blue cap protruding from behind the jack pine.

The old fool, Gordon thought angrily. The stubborn old Swedish fool! He'll just get us both clawed up. You can't reason with him. It's like trying to move a boulder ten times bigger than you are. He's going to make me shoot, and I'm sure to miss. What can I do?

Shoot as well as you can, Gordon's mind told him. What else now? And what was it that Lars had said about readiness? "Readiness is only way to prepare for danger." Well, the least he could do was to get his gun ready. Hastily he removed the safety catch, and in misery he waited.

At first he could hear nothing but the brooding mountain silence, but soon the muffled sounds from the willow clump came again: the crack of an occasional dead branch and the tearing slash of the bear's claws as it dug out grubs. His flesh shuddered at the thought of those sharp, tearing claws and the power behind them. What if—? But he'd better not think about those claws. Tension stiffening his body until his muscles hurt, he watched the willows.

Minutes that seemed hours went by on slow feet. Once he thought he saw a moving gray shadow low among the brush. The bear was coming out! He tightened his grip on his gun, raised it slowly. But the gray shadow stayed in the willows, going noisily about its feeding again, and he lowered his gun in relief.

A willful October breeze swooped over the opposite canyon wall and whirled downward to attack the tips of the aspen trees. The last stubborn golden leaves danced and struggled and then gave up to drift slowly down to the snows. The breeze romped off up the ridge, and silence shut down. Even the bear was quiet now. Gordon felt as if he must shout to break the stillness, but just when he thought he could stand the waiting no longer, a loud swishing and crashing came from the willows. The bear had finished its feeding. It was coming now.

Hastily Gordon raised his rifle again, and it shook in his hands. He looked over at the blue cap and white hair behind the jack pine and saw the barrel of the trapper's gun rise slowly. He steadied his own shaking rifle against a protruding knot of aspen and took aim at the place from which he judged the bear might emerge from the willows. Watching tensely, he tried to control the shivering of his body that shook his gun.

He saw the great gray animal lumber heavily but swiftly from the end of the willow clump. The breeze swept down again from the canyon wall, across the bear, across the hunters, and off up the ridge behind them. Although the wind was right, the bear seemed instinctively to sense peril. It stopped abruptly, stood motionless, looked around, its huge shaggy head turning from side to side as if trying to see danger. Then it rose on its hind feet, evidently in an effort to look over a larger area. The big gray body was turned slightly toward Gordon, heart side exposed as if asking for death.

"It's a good shot," Gordon muttered to himself.

Again he aimed, but his gun shook too much for accurate sighting. He dared not shoot. What was it Lars had said? "When something have to be done, then you will do it." Queer—the shaking had stopped. The gun barrel was steady. Gordon aimed again. He pulled the trigger, and the shot rang out.

The bear's great forepaws clawed the air. It staggered from the impact of the bullet, fell to the ground, lay still.

"Lars!" Gordon shouted. "Lars! I got him! I got him!"

Forgetful of caution, he started to run toward the gray mound.

"Come back! Come back! Keep away!" Lars shouted.

But Gordon did not even hear the warning shout. He did not hear the pounding run of the old trapper's feet behind him. All he knew was that he had killed a bear. He did remember to hold his gun ready for another shot if it should be needed, and he slowed to a walk as he neared the bear.

The gray heap stirred. Gordon stopped abruptly. He had not killed the thing after all. Quickly he aimed his gun, pulled the trigger in frantic haste, but in his excitement he had forgotten to throw the lever of his gun to renew the cartridge. Fifteen feet away from him, the gray heap that should have been lifeless scrambled to its four feet, shook its great head, and growled in anger and in pain.

"Run!" Gordon heard from close beside him. "Run!" He wanted to obey, to run as he never had run before. But something was wrong: he could not move. Ice, cold and hard, seemed to hold him rigid. Muscles refused the command of brain. Dimly he saw the bear rise, swaying, to its hind feet, saw the huge forepaws clawing air, heard the roars, deep and angry, rolling from its throat.

Run, Gordon told his legs. But the legs were wooden posts rooted in hard and rocky soil. Lars was beside him now, a shadow in a dream. Why didn't he shoot? Why didn't he kill this death that threatened? What was he waiting for? And then the shot came.

But the bear did not fall! Roused to fury by new pain, it staggered toward its enemies. Head lowered for the charge, huge forepaws raised to slash, it came on until Gordon could see the inside of the great mouth with its yellow fangs, sharp and cruel. Eyes fixed in horror, he waited for death.

The bear was almost at the point of his gun barrel, the stock still held rigidly in stiffened hands, when there came another shot. The shaggy beast swayed, staggered, dropped from the range of Gordon's glazed stare.

"We got him, boy. This time the bear is dead," he heard Lars say as if from a long way off.

III

*G*ordon *stood frozen,* still unable to move. He felt an arm around his shoulders, heard Lars say, "Come now. You must walk over to that log. Walk."

Gordon knew when the gun was taken gently from stiff fingers. He felt a supporting arm around his waist and found that he could make his legs move, although the rest of his body stayed rigid. Stiffly, mechanically, he walked. He was grateful when Lars helped him down to the log, grateful for the talk that went on and on, soothingly. Slowly the stiffened muscles relaxed.

"I have ask too much of you," Lars was saying. "Nature have build us to take only so much. Big scare is like big pain—when comes too much, mind go blank and body freeze."

Gordon felt ill with shame. He put his head stiffly down on his knees and, face hidden, muttered, "I was scared all right. I guess I must be a coward."

"No, boy, no. All brave men have the big scare at some time. Brave man fears—and stands. Coward runs away. You did not run."

"Run? I couldn't run. Probably would have, if I could have moved."

Lars chuckled. "Comes time when man should run. But

you run wrong way at wrong time—right toward the bear. It is good to face danger, but it is folly to run toward sure death. You didn't wait to see if bear was killed."

"Then it looks as if I'm both a fool and a coward."

"Foolish, yes. Coward, no. I will prove it to you. When you aim the first time, your gun shake, and I know you have bad scare. But when you have sighted, then hand and gun grow steady. Coward keep on shaking, maybe run. But brave man, when come time for steady, then he has the quiet mind and the strength he need. Maybe he still have the fright, but he does not let it stop him. So! Then he act. Then is he brave man."

Gordon grinned ruefully. "I don't feel very brave. Look at me. I'm shaking again right now."

"That is result come after big emotion—reaction. We will go see to our bear, and you will get over it."

When he stood over the lifeless mass of gray fur, Gordon looked down at it feeling ill with a distaste that he tried to cover by asking, "What do we do with the thing now? Is the meat any good?"

"Not from this bear. He have too many year. Too big. But the pelt—your mother would like it, nice and warm for her floor. See, he is Silvertip. Hair is brown near the skin, but each hair have tip of silver. Come, we will skin him."

"How—how do we go about it?"

"Bear which is fresh killed is ungainly to handle—like a bowl of jelly." Lars laughed. "This one is mighty heavy jelly. Weigh four hundred, five hundred pound. We must roll him over."

Gordon did not want to touch the carcass and he made no move to help. Lars looked up, but did not say anything, only knelt at the bear's head and began skinning, talking quietly as he worked. "See, I think this is where your bullet struck. It crease the side of his head, stun him. That is when he fall the first time."

"Well, at least my shot hit him," Gordon said, stooping over to inspect the wound, proud because he had shared in bringing down the bear.

Lars talked cheerfully on, explaining the steps in the skinning process as he worked at it, and soon, without knowing when he began, Gordon was helping.

Lars nodded with satisfaction. "Good. Now we roll him over." And Gordon found that he no longer dreaded touching the shaggy carcass. The old man smiled, nodding again. "That the bear no longer make you feel ill—that is good too. It is like in my country, when skier fall on jump, he climb right back up the hill and try again. He get used that way to what he have not wished to do. Man is not born brave, Gordon. He make courage for himself by training."

The sun was halfway down the western sky before they finished their task. Lars folded and rolled the skin, and the two of them together carried it back to the aspens where the horses were tethered.

"I will put the pelt on my saddle," Lars said. "Your Lance would only be bolting. My old Thor, he will not like, but he has carried bear before. I will walk."

"We'll both walk," Gordon insisted.

Dark clouds rolled up to cover the sun, and as they tramped across the mesa, snow flurries began to swirl down from the peaks. By the time they reached the ranch corral at dusk, snow was falling steadily. Molly, her pigtails flying, came running out of the house.

"Did you get the bear?" she called. And then when she saw them walking and the mound of gray lashed on a saddle, she jumped up and down, burbling her words in her excitement. "Oh, Lars! Oh, Gordy! You did. You got him.

And the fur's gray! Then it was really a grizzly. Did you shoot him, Gordy?"

Gordon laughed. "Me? Nope. It took a better man than I am to bring home this bearskin. Lars got him, of course. I hit him though. Creased his head and stunned him."

"Did you? Good for you, Gordy. I knew you would. Unroll the skin quick and let me see the claws. Where was he? What was he doing? What did he do when you shot him? Did he come at you?"

"The little Molly, she wants to know all things at one time," Lars said, laughing at her. "Run back to the cabin, girl, and we will be in as soon as we put up the horses. Then Gordon will answer all the questions you have ask so fast. Run now. You will be cold. You have no coat."

"Pfoo, what's a little bit of cold—when Gordy and you have just shot a bear? Let me see a little of it, Gordy. Please."

Happy because he had restored her pride in him, he unrolled a corner of the skin to let her see one of the huge paws. "There," he said. "Now look."

"If it please you, Molly," Lars offered, "I will carry the skin in to show your good mother. We will give Jean a chance to get her cry over before Gordon comes in. I will come back to help put up the horses."

When the two hunters came in out of the storm, Molly had the bearskin spread on the kitchen floor and was down on her knees examining the claws, but Gordon saw that his mother's face looked sick and white in the light from the lamp. She did not say much, only, "Oh, Gordy," and then she turned away and busied herself at the stove.

"You have brave boy, Jean," Lars remarked reprovingly. "You should have pride in him for helping shoot this bear."

"I didn't do much," Gordon put in honestly. "Lars was the one who shot it. I was—"

Lars shook his head, for they had agreed to keep the real details from her. She turned from the stove, trying to smile.

"I am proud of my son," she said. "It's only that— Do take the monster's skin out of here, Gordy, now that we've seen it. There's weather making, Lars. You must stay the night. Supper will be ready by the time Gordon finishes the milking, and the coffeepot is waiting on the stove right now."

The trapper sniffed the good odors of roasting mutton and saw the loaves of fresh bread on the kitchen table. "I will stay, Jean, but first I will help Gordon milk."

"No, no, Lars," Molly insisted eagerly. "You stay in by the fire. I'll help Gordy. I'll make him tell me all about shooting the bear. Mother doesn't want to hear because thinking about the bear makes her feel ill. But I do. You'll tell me, won't you, Gordy?"

He took up the milk pails and a lantern and waited for Molly to shrug into her jacket. He was a little hurt by the way his mother had acted. Probably she'd been going around all day thinking that he'd get slashed or killed. He was glad that Molly wanted to hear the story, glad because she didn't care whether it was he or Lars who had shot the bear, but he wasn't going to tell her about his freezing up when the bear came at him. That near disaster was to be a secret between Lars and him.

When they came back from the barn, supper was steaming on the table. Lars turned the talk to the ranch work.

"You have the readiness for winter when the snow comes deep?" he asked Gordon.

"Not everything. The hay is stacked in the feeding meadow beside the cattle shelter, but the cattle are still up on the range. I've got to bring them down soon. There's enough wood to last until spring. The barn roof needs mending. We have some salt meat, but I'd like to get a few deer so we'll have venison to help out and I won't have to butcher too many sheep."

"We will make a bargain, Gordon," Lars offered. "I have plenty venison laid by, but I will help you with hunting, if you will sometimes help me with my trapping."

Gordon thought of his difficulty with skis, but he hated to mention it to Lars, who skied so well. Out in the barn there was an old pair of snowshoes—webs the valley people called them, and they called skis snowshoes. There were the skis his father had made also, but Gordon thought he'd do better on the webs. Clumsy things they were, and yet they were safe and sure.

"Well," he said, "I don't know much about trapping, but I'd like to learn. And I could certainly use help with my hunting."

Lars nodded. "It is a bargain we have made then. And we should be hunting the deer now before the snows get too deep. Soon they will be leaving for low country. We could go tomorrow, Gordon, perhaps bring home enough to last you through the winter. Would you like that?"

"I sure would. Shooting deer will just be fun after that bear today. Shall we—?"

"Oh, Lars, Gordy, may I go too?" Molly interrupted. "Let me go. You made me stay home today."

Warm in the knowledge that his sister had welcomed him back into her favor, Gordon nodded. "Sure you can go. Hunting deer isn't dangerous like going after bear." Then he saw his mother shaking her head at him, and regretfully he began backing down. "No, maybe you'd better not. We—we might have to camp out in the forest overnight, and it'll be cold and wet."

"I wouldn't mind," Molly persisted. "I can do it if you can."

"I know you could," Gordon went on, unhappy because he hated to refuse her. "But there's Mother. She'd be all alone. Nobody to help her with the milking."

Molly glanced quickly at her mother and did not beg any more, but as she rose to clear the table, she muttered something about "boys having all the fun," and she clattered the dishes with unnecessary noise and splashed water into the dishpan. Her mother noticed and, smiling sympathetically, went to help. Gordon and Lars moved from the table to sit beside the fireplace, where fir logs sputtered into flame that roared up the big chimney.

"It will not be necessary—the camping," Lars said. "I have good friend, Old Tom, which have cabin high in mountains. He will be happy to have us stay the night with him."

"You mean Tom Rider? That old prospector who has a cabin on Beaver Creek? I know him. He stops here sometimes on his way to his diggings, and Mother feeds him."

"Yes, that is him. Old Tom."

"Old Tom?" Mother asked, hearing the name. "He's a queer person." She left Molly to finish the dishes and brought mending to the fire.

"Tom is very gentle man," Lars said. "Queer, perhaps, but good."

"I know he is," Mother agreed. "The first time he came tramping in here with that big pack on his back, I didn't know quite how to take him. He was so rough looking—and whiskery. Dirty, too. But he was sweet and kind, so pleased with everything I did for him that now I'm always glad to see him coming. They have a lonely life, these prospectors."

"Not lonely, Jean," Lars said, chuckling. "They like aloneness in the mountains. Old Tom is happy man—have dog to talk to, warm cabin, gun for meat, and always the hope that someday he will find the big riches."

"Perhaps so, but I wouldn't like such a life. Well, anyway, if you and Gordy plan to stay the night with Old Tom, you must take him a loaf of my fresh bread and some newly churned butter."

The next morning promised a bright day, for the night's storm clouds were rolling off to the north. It was still dawn dusk when Lars and Gordon rode out of the gate, leading the work team and another saddle horse to carry back the three deer that Lars hoped to get. He turned his black gelding toward the lofty barrier of the range, its wind-swept crags a dark misty blue in the dim light. New white covered the lower slopes, and down in the valley the night's storm had left two inches of fresh snow that was "just right for hunting deer," Lars said.

They forded the clear waters of the Salmon River, scarcely more than a creek here so near its birthplace, and turned their horses toward the forested foothills, lying like a dark green scalloped belt in front of the barren domes and spires of the range. Lars hunted until he found a narrow path angling off through the sagebrush.

"This is Tom's trail," he explained.

Gordon was excited and happy because this was the first time he ever had gone on a long hunting trip. That first year on the ranch there had been time only for necessities because he and his father had been busy grubbing the sagebrush from the flat, planting the quick-growing timothy for hay, digging the long ditch that brought water to the meadows from the spring in the hills. In the fall they had hunted for deer in the gulches back of the barn, shooting all they needed. Gordon knew that Lars had proposed the two-day trip only because he wanted to visit his friend Tom before the winter snows hemmed all the mountain people in their cabins.

The old trapper paused before they entered the forest and pointed a gloved hand down the valley with its tremendous wall of guarding peaks. "A lifetime," he said, "would not be enough years to find all the beauties hiding in this wilderness. Up there lakes bluer than skies have hide themselves. Forests so thick no man can push through. Animals living as they have for hundreds of years. To be alone with all this—that is good for spirit of man."

"Maybe, but all it does for me is to make me feel sort of—trapped. It takes strength to fight a country tough like this one."

"Strength, yes. But who would be weak? This valley, these mountains have strength to give the strong. The weak they destroy. Only the strong can live here."

"I guess I'm not strong then," Gordon said stubbornly. "It's too lonely."

Lars made no answer, but turned his horse into the mouth of the trail that cut a narrow cavern into deep pine forest. Gordon followed, knowing that his friend disapproved of him.

The trail opened out after a time into a small mountain meadow, its long grasses sered to amber by the early frosts. Golden brown was the grass, and golden in the sunlight were the hides of a small doe and her dappled fawn, its delicate hoofs moving close beside its mother. Automatically Gordon raised his rifle.

"No," Lars said sharply. "Let her go."

The doe lifted a startled head, saw the intruders, and bounded gracefully into the timber, the fawn leaping after her.

"Why pass up a good chance like that?" Gordon asked.

"Doe which raise young have right to life," Lars answered, softening reproof with a smile.

"Sure. I knew that. I just didn't think. Too eager to get venison, I guess."

"We will find plenty bucks for our guns," Lars said as they crossed the sunny meadow to enter the dim light of forest trail again.

The path came out soon on a hillside where the pines thinned, and below Gordon saw another meadow with a stream running through underbrush. "Isn't this a good place?" he asked. "The snow's gone in spots, and there's grass for deer. The wind's right too."

Lars nodded. "Yes. We will wait here. Soon deer will come."

They found a log free of snow and sat down to wait, rifles ready for quick sighting. Gordon was beginning to grow restless when he heard a rustling in the forest across the narrow meadow, and out of the pines stepped a good-sized buck, fat and sleek-furred. He crossed a snowy patch, drank from the stream and then, leaping across the water, moved toward the bare sunny spots in the meadow.

"Shall I shoot?" Gordon whispered, raising his gun.

"No. Watch," Lars whispered back, putting out a restraining hand. "He is young buck. Maybe you see a wonder."

Feeling the good warm sun, the buck tossed his new antlers and jumped up into the air, coming down to strike the ground with four feet close together. He lowered his head, rushed a small pine tree with his antlers, several times as if attacking an enemy. Jumping again into the air, he came down to leap about the glade in wild glee, stopping suddenly as he passed the hunters' hiding place. Great soft eyes looked into Gordon's own. But the buck only stood still as if surprised, as if he never had seen man before and did not sense the danger they brought. Lars gave a sharp whistle. The buck threw up his head and Lars fired his rifle, a clean shot that put a bullet in the neck.

"Lars, how could you?" Gordon cried, running to kneel beside the fallen deer. "After he put on that dance for us?"

"I know how you feel," Lars explained, "but your mother have need of venison. It was too good a shot to lose. Need is only excuse, ever, for killing anything beautiful like deer, and harmless. Shoot the deer only when meat is necessity, and never more than can be used."

Gordon knew that Lars was right and sensible. Death for the deer, the cutting off of life in the midst of happy play, seemed hard and cruel, but the meat that his mother had bought was not enough to last the winter. Butchering the sheep or some of the calves would cut down the herds and must be avoided. The hunters prepared the deer for packing back to the ranch, hanging the carcass in a tree near the trail to pick up on their return.

As they rode on, Gordon asked, "What was the deer doing? All that dancing around?"

"It is the buck dance. He feel good, this buck, happy before deep snows have come to make hard the winter living. He practice with antlers because he want to drive some other buck away from does. That way he get does for himself. Buck dance is wilderness sight."

After watching the buck cavorting wild and free in the meadow, Gordon wondered if he could ever shoot deer again, but he did, for they came upon a herd of seven feeding in another meadow. There were two bucks, an old one and a very young one without antlers.

"You take big one," Lars whispered.

Remembering only the necessity of his family, Gordon steadied his gun and shot. Each hunter brought down his buck, and the does leaped off alone into the brush.

"Look, Lars, mine's a big one," Gordon exulted, running to his deer. "Four-point antlers."

"Yes, he is old one. Mine is young—spike buck."

"What's that? Spike buck?"

"Always you find only one buck to each bunch of doe, unless second one is very young. See, mine so young he have only spike for antler. That is why your old one have not run him off for jealousy. Pretty soon old one fight young one off and have does all to himself. Then maybe later come along another strong young buck, like one which dance. Old one is getting too old, and young one fight him and kill. Then strong one gets does."

"Let's not shoot any more deer," Gordon suggested, because knowing the habits of deer made them seem human to him. "Three's enough. Let's dress these out and hang them and then ride on to Old Tom's."

It seemed to him that they traveled for miles up and up the forest trail that climbed through pines so dense that the sun could not melt the snow from the path. They crossed and recrossed small streams and detoured or jumped their horses over fallen trees. Sometimes through clearings in the pines they glimpsed the peaks, overpoweringly close now, for they were well into the edge of the range. Once they came upon a small lake, emerald green in the shadow of the pines. In waters so clear that Gordon could see logs and rocks deep down on the bottom, a snowy peak looked at itself as in a mirror. In the center of the lake big white birds swam in stately splendor.

"Trumpeter swans," Lars whispered. "Watch."

The leaders knew that the hunters were there, and twice the males trumpeted to their mates. Flapping wings fast and hard, the swans swam to the upper end of the lake, six small blue birds paddling and fluttering valiantly beside their mothers.

"They're trying to rise," Gordon whispered.

"Yes. Watch."

The swans had reached the upper end of the lake, but their feet were still in water, their wings dipping. They rose, cleared the lake but had not enough elevation to fly above the trees. Circling, they came down again to the lake, white wings reflected in emerald waters. Again they circled, a hundred feet high this time. On the third circle the leaders aimed for a low ridge to the south and, topping it, flew off, forming a white arrowhead against the sky.

Gordon drew in his breath sharply at the sheer beauty he had seen. "I've watched trumpeter flights high in the sky, but I never was this close before. What do they call the young swans?"

"Cygnets. Soon their feathers will turn white." Lars smiled. "The wilderness you do not like is treating you well today. It is late for trumpeter swan. Usually they fly in September. Tonight they will find another lake."

The mountains were gun-metal gray against a yellow sky when they rode at last into the small clearing and saw Old Tom's cabin, but, although it was dusk there in the shadows of the pines, no lights shone from the cabin's one small window. No cheerful blue smoke rose from the chimney.

"Looks as if Old Tom isn't home," Gordon said. "Guess we'll have to cook our own dinner."

An old brown hound, white-spotted, rose growling from the carcass of a fawn that it had been gnawing and ran into the forest.

"Tom's dog. Old King," Lars said, dismounting. He turned the fawn over with his foot, looking worried. "This is not Tom's work. He would not kill a fawn. His dog have gone wild—running deer. Something is wrong."

Finding the door unlocked, they pushed in. The cabin

was dark and airless, but enough of dusky light filtered through dirty windowpanes to show Old Tom stretched silent on the bed.

"Tom, are you ill?" Lars called out. He walked to the still figure on the bed and stood looking down. "It is no use to ask Tom," he told Gordon. "See, my old friend knew he was going. He have laid him decently on his bed to wait for death. It has not been long, I think. A day, two day, maybe."

Gordon found that he was trembling with a feeling he could not master, not the frozen terror with which he had faced the charging bear, but a shrinking dismay, a distrust of something he could not understand—the mystery of death.

IV

Lars drew the soiled blanket over the face of his friend and picked up from the cover a slip of paper on which words were scrawled in pencil.

"Read what Tom has written," Lars said, handing the note to Gordon. "I am slow at reading the English."

Gordon carried the paper to the light from the window and read aloud, trying to keep his voice from trembling:

> "Lars—I have struck it rich but it aint goin to do me no good. You know why. aint got nobody to leave it to so you take it. in the tree—you know where—is a map so you can find it. take keer of my old dog king. clame is staked but aint filed."

The signature began with a wavering capital T and ran off into nothingness. Ill with emotion, for this was the first time he had seen death, Gordon handed the note back, the paper fluttering in his hand. The old trapper smiled serenely.

"You have fear for this husk my old friend Tom have leave behind?" Lars asked softly. "Do not do so. It have no power to harm. In life Tom was good man. Save your distaste for that living man whose mind and spirit hold evil." When Gordon did not answer, Lars went on in a matter-of-fact tone. "We must bury my friend where he ask me to, the last time I visit him. On the little hill behind the cabin."

Glad to be doing something, Gordon found a shovel and pick outside and carried them with a lantern up the hill. When he returned to the cabin, Lars had rolled Old Tom in a blanket, and they lifted their burden and carried it toward the lantern's gleam. King came from the forest to follow, whimpering, at their heels.

"Here is the place under this big tree," Lars said, and they laid the blanket-wrapped figure down in the snow. "Tom knew his old heart was refusing its work, that he must soon die. I have tell him. It is why I have come here today —to see if my friend still live."

Three hours it took them to dig a grave in the frozen soil before they could lower Old Tom into his resting place. Lars said a brief prayer for his friend.

"Please, God," he said, "take back my good friend Tom, which never have evil thought in all his life. This Tom is wilderness man. If You can do so, please give him mountains and timber. Maybe ore to dig. Old prospector need digging to make happy, and Tom have deserve that happiness."

In Swedish, Lars spoke more words, and although Gordon could not understand them, he knew they formed a prayer from the way Lars said them. After that, they put the earth back into the grave and rolled a flat rock across for a headstone. King lay down beside the mound, head on his forepaws.

"Let him be for now," Lars said. "We will go back now to the cabin, Gordon. You will forget soon, but I will remember this good man for long time. Do not feel sadness because death have taken Tom. Death is an end, yes. But sometimes it come as a friend, and it was so for Tom, I think."

Finding relief from his thoughts in work, Gordon chopped wood from the pile outside the cabin and carried in an armload of split kindlings. He found a leg of venison hanging in the lean-to and took the haunch into the cabin and then, still not wanting to stay in the cheerless room, walked to the little meadow to check the horses he had hobbled there. When he returned to the cabin, Lars had tidied and aired it and was now busily scouring out the coffeepot.

"Tom was good man, but he wasn't always clean," the trapper remarked cheerfully. "When I come to see him, always I must scour the pot."

In the lamplight, with the fire crackling cheerfully in the sheet iron stove and the battered kettle beginning to sing, the cabin seemed less gloomy to Gordon. For supper there were venison steaks, the fresh bread they had brought with them, tinned peaches from Tom's supply shelf, and coffee, hot and strong. After he had eaten, Gordon began to feel himself again, but suddenly Tom's hound dog startled him with a long and eerie howl from outside the door.

"Old King!" he exclaimed. "He's come back. We've been forgetting him. Maybe he'll make friends with us now."

He went outside and sat down on the doorstep, leaving the door open behind him. King retreated to the edge of the timber, whimpering. Gordon sat silent for a time and then he began to call softly to the dog. Several times King crept close, belly to ground, only to slink whining back to the forest. Gordon sat on. Finally the dog came and lay down beside the step as if unable to resist human companionship. Gordon paid no attention at first, but soon he put out a hand and gently scratched behind the hound's flopping ears. Quietly he talked to King, explaining as to a person the reason for the master's absence. When Gordon rose to enter the cabin, King crept in at his heels.

The dog only sniffed at the food offered and then turned away to settle stiffly down behind the stove on a piece of sacking, evidently his bed. Whimpering occasionally, head on forepaws, King watched the two intruders as they washed the dishes. The sad hound eyes followed every movement and seemed to say that these two must now be his friends, since the old friend had gone away.

All the time that Gordon was wiping the dishes, he kept thinking about the note Old Tom had left. Lars seemed to have forgotten about it, but he, too, must have been curious, for when the last dish was put away, he said, "Bring me the note, Gordon. We must read it again. Old Tom have left a trust for us."

Eagerly Gordon took the note from behind the clock on the shelf, where it had been placed for safekeeping. With growing excitement, he read the letter aloud again.

"The tree?" he asked. "What did Old Tom mean about this tree you're supposed to know?"

"It is hollow tree—down by creek. There I have leave note for Tom when I come, and he is not home."

"But, look here, he says there's a map in it. Let's go and get it right now. Maybe the ore he found is really good. And then you'd be rich, Lars, because he left it to you. Let's take the lantern and go find that map."

Lars grumbled something about how late it was and about an old man needing rest after long labor, but he rose from the table and lit the lantern. When they started out the door, King stirred himself to follow his new friends, as if he dared not let them get away from him. Lars went down a little hill to the creek that flowed, seemingly in a circle, around the cabin.

"Here it is—the tree," he said stopping before a huge pine that had been blasted by lightning in some long-ago summer storm. "Hold the lantern high, and I will see what Tom have left for us."

Breathlessly Gordon watched as Lars felt around in a deep hole in the tree trunk. What if there was nothing there? What if Old Tom had only been having the dreams of illness, had made it all up out of his sick fancies? But in a minute Lars pulled out a small dirty buckskin bag.

"Oh, quick, Lars. Look inside. How can you be so slow?"

Lars laughed. "You are impatient, like the little Molly. We will wait until we get back to the cabin where light will be better."

On the kitchen table he placed the bag, and with maddening deliberation he opened it to pull out a piece of folded paper.

"Is it a map?" Gordon asked, scarcely able to keep from snatching the paper. "What's on it? Hurry, Lars. Golly, this is just like *Treasure Island* that Molly and I have been reading. Hidden treasure. Maps and things. What's on it, Lars? Tell me."

Lars handed him the paper, and there wasn't any map. "Why, it's nothing but some directions," Gordon said, disappointed.

"Directions will do. Read them to me."

"Whew," Gordon exclaimed, "Old Tom sure couldn't spell." Stumbling a little in his excitement then, he read aloud:

"Lars—X crick by blased tree then walk 10 paces strate ahed. turn s. by e. at big bolder and walk 23 paces til you com to small gulch. X at down tree. turn sharp left for 52 paces then X second gulch with crick. climb e. bank and work acros to n. e. You will find tunel hole in rock wall. stakes mark clame. I think ore is rich."

Lars puffed at his pipe and thought. "Is easy once we find blazed tree," he said.

"Let's start right now. Please, Lars. I can't wait."

"No. It is late, and this old man is tired. We get up early in morning. Find mine then."

Gordon was disappointed, but without arguing he helped Lars hunt for extra blankets. It was difficult to think of Lars as an old man, but, after all, it had been a hard day for him—the long ride, burying his friend. He settled himself on the bed, and Gordon piled some old pelts on the floor in front of the stove and rolled up in a comforter, but he could not sleep for thinking of Old Tom and the claim he had left. King crawled close, thumping his tail on the floor, and Gordon reached out to stroke the dog's head. Tom's tin clock, which Lars had started, ticked loudly, an owl screeched in the timber, and King growled softly. Gordon went to sleep at last to dream that he was lost in a dark tunnel and that he was pouring nuggets of gold through his fingers.

In the morning he woke to the rattling of stove lids and the smell of coffee. Lars was up and the fire was crackling merrily, driving the night chill from the air.

"I'll go get a bucket of water," Gordon offered.

There was slush ice in the swift-flowing stream when he filled his bucket. Winter's coming, he thought, and if we don't find that claim today, maybe we can't get up here again until spring.

After a breakfast of more venison steaks, he took out the directions and read them again. "'X crick by blased tree,'" he read aloud. "Well, looks as if the first thing to do is to find the blaze. Ought to be easy."

Lars chuckled. "I think—not easy. Two streams flow around this cabin on its hill. We do not know on which creek is blazed tree."

"Then we'll have to search both. Let's get started. You take one stream, and I'll take the other."

Tom's cabin was built on a hill that thrust itself, ridge-like, from a steep mountainside. A creek dropped swiftly, evidently from some hidden lake above, the stream dividing when it struck the hill and sending a channel down each side of the cabin. Above and to the east, when they went outside, they could see another rivulet pouring over a high, rocky projection to fall in cascades through a rocky gulch. Behind them, across the little meadow, they could hear the music of still another stream.

Lars scratched his white head in bewilderment. Then he remarked hopefully, "That creek to the east—she come down gulch. Tom's letter say after we cross first creek we come to gulch. Maybe we save time to look there?"

"No good, Lars. Last night when I was up in the meadow where the horses are, I saw a gulch down that side too."

"Creeks up, creeks down, creeks all over mountain," Lars remarked ruefully. "Gulch all over too."

Gordon, too, was puzzled, but after a moment's thought he said slowly, "Lars, look. It's reasonable to explore these two streams near the cabin. The forest is thick beyond the clearing, and there's heavy underbrush. Tom would know that you wouldn't have an idea where to begin unless he gave you a good tip. And if he'd put his mark on one of the second creeks, I think he'd have said so."

Lars nodded. "You make sense, boy. So?"

"So, we start hunting nearby. You take the west stream. That one to the east looks pretty rough—lots of clamber-ing around over rocks. I'll take it."

For three or four hours they searched, but when Lars hallooed to bring Gordon back to the cabin, neither one had found any sign of a blazed tree.

"Old Tom have tricked us," Lars said, chuckling. "He give me his mine, but he not want me or any one else to find hidden riches in great hurry." He frowned then. "I do not understand why he do this. Something is—not right."

Gordon was unwilling to give up. "Maybe we missed the blaze. Maybe he made it pretty small. Let's take another look."

"No. We must go back to the ranch now. Morning is almost gone."

"We can't. We just can't, Lars. Not until we find that blaze. There's time because—well, we'll get down a lot faster than we rode up."

Lars glanced up at the clouding sky. "We will need to. A storm comes. Besides, your mother will worry by dark if we are not home."

"But we just have to find that claim now. If it snows—"

"The ore—it does not have legs," Lars said firmly. "It will not rise up and walk away. Tom's riches will stay fast in rock and wait for us to come again. We will go now."

Gordon knew that when his friend spoke in that tone, further protests were useless, and he took out his exasperation in chopping more wood and kindling to pile beside the stove. After a hasty lunch of leftover food, he rehung the venison in the lean-to and swept out the cabin while Lars washed the dishes.

"Shouldn't we nail up the door and windows?" Gordon asked.

"No. Some prospector or hunter might have need for shelter and food and warmth to save life. In mountains always leave cabin unlocked and clean, with food for the next man. Come, we must go."

When they were on their horses and ready to start, Gordon called to King, but the old dog lay down on the doorstep, whined, and refused to move.

"We can't leave him," Gordon said. "You try, Lars. You need a dog anyway, now that your old collie is gone."

"You do not want King?" Lars asked.

"But I do—only—well, Pete would probably chew him up. Pete's young and sort of jealous."

"And King is old—yes?" Lars nodded, smiling. "Old dog is better with old man." He dismounted and went back to the hound. Gently he petted the head that lifted to his hand, talked softly. "Come, King. You know that your good friend and mine is gone. He will not come again. I will be friend now. If hungry, feed. If sleepy, nice warm place by my fire. I your friend now, you mine. Come, King."

The dog rose stiffly to his feet, sniffed at the crack of the cabin door, whined once, and then turned to follow Lars as if in understanding of the old man's words.

They rode down the mountain, resting occasionally for King's sake and stopping at the meadows to load the carcasses of the deer on the spare horses. As they started on again, the sky grew darker, and by the time they had reached the road across the flat, the occasional snow flurries had turned into a steady storm.

Gordon turned up his coat collar to keep out the fast-falling flakes and remarked disconsolately, "If this is staying snow, we'll never get back to find Tom's claim."

"Snow do not need to keep us away. We can ski to find our mine. You can ski, Gordon?"

"Not very well. I can get around on the fool things and slide downhill some. Climbing and walking on the flat is just plain work, and I don't like going fast. Molly's better than I am. She likes speed. And if she lands in a snowbank, she just laughs and calls it fun. I don't. I guess I don't like skiing."

"I will teach you to ski right. So. You go down fast. Go uphill and on flat—and not too much work."

"Would you, Lars? I'd like that—I think. Molly would, I know. And I guess if I'm going to help you trap, I've got to be better on skis than I am now. How long have you skied, Lars? To get as good on them as you are?"

"Always. In Sweden, up north where I have lived, babies learn to walk on ski. Go to school on ski. Snow there last ten month, sometimes more."

"Golly! That's worse than here. The snows are what I hate about this valley."

"I teach you joy of the ski. Then you will like time when come snow. You will feel only pleasure when you see ahead big mountain of snow which drop down and down."

Gordon didn't quite like the picture of himself poised on the brink of endless down-dropping snows. It might be fun to learn to ski well enough so that he could get around better on the hills near the ranch, he decided, but that was as far as he wanted to go with this skiing business. He thought that it was time to talk of other things.

"What did you do, Lars, before you came to America? In Sweden, I mean. Back there—when we buried Old Tom—you said that you had told him he had heart trouble. How did you know?"

"I have study to be a doctor for a little time, but I do not like it because I was too much inside. I try many things—a little business, teach school—"

"Teach school? Do you know algebra? Could you teach me—this winter when there isn't much ranch work to do? Could you, Lars?"

"I think so. The figures, they are easy for me."

"Golly, Lars, that would be great. If I could go on learning, maybe I wouldn't mind. I like math, and Mother's not much good at it. Of course, she can teach us English, and we get large doses of literature and history, both Molly and me."

"You have the algebra book?" Lars asked.

"Yes. When my teacher heard that I couldn't come back to school she sent me some textbooks, and one of them was an algebra. It was too much for either Mother or me. Molly's awfully dumb at figures, too, like Mother. If you could help us—"

"I will help. I will be like rusty hammer at first, but even rusty hammer can maybe pound in knowledge."

"Maybe it won't take too much pounding. What else did you do in Sweden, Lars?"

"Always I like outdoors and mountains. So I turn guide. People in my country like touring in mountains on ski, and I take them. It was a life and work that I like, and I do it long time back. Then—I come to this country."

Gordon knew that the mountain people seldom inquired into the past of any man who came to live in the valley, but there was one more question he wanted answered. He hesitated a moment and then asked, "If you were happy in your work, Lars, then why did you come to America?"

The old trapper did not reply at once. Stopping his horse at the ranch gate, he turned in his saddle to look back at the peaks, their summits almost hidden in dusk and swirling snow.

Finally Lars said quietly: "That is something I do not like to talk about, but I will tell you now. So. We will not again mention. I have good wife in Sweden, but we have no children. She—died. Then I do not wish to stay there more. I come to this country, hunt until I find this valley. Snow. Mountains. Like Sweden. I stay here now—until I die. Like Old Tom."

"Oh, Lars," Gordon said. "I—I'm sorry."

In silence they rode on to the corral, put up their horses, hung the deer under the shed roof, and walked to the house. Gordon was grieved because he had caused his friend pain, but he was glad that he knew more about Lars. Understanding made friendship warmer.

V

The cabin windows were blurs of golden light through the soft-falling snow as the hunters walked from the barn. Molly heard their voices, and the taller oblong of the door, as she opened it, shone suddenly yellow.

"Did you get the deer, Gordy?" she called.

"Three. All we need. I shot a big buck."

"I knew you would, Gordy." Molly nodded in satisfaction and went on breathlessly. "Supper's waiting. Come on in, Lars."

"We'll take King in too," Gordon told Lars. "Mother won't mind. He'd be lonesome outside, and he's too old to fight off Pete." For the shepherd was growling and bristling at the stranger.

King followed them to stand just inside the door as if asking whether it was right to enter. His eyes begged understanding.

"Oh, where did you get him, Gordy?" Molly asked. "Whose dog is he, Lars?"

"This is King. Old Tom's dog," Lars explained. "My friend Tom is dead."

Jean Stevens turned from the stove to say softly, "I'm sorry, Lars. You will miss Tom. We all will." After a small silence, she went on, "Bring King in to the fire. He looks sad and tired."

Molly went down on her knees beside the hound, laying her cheek against the flopping ears. "Don't be lonely, King, old boy. I love you."

The dog nudged his head against her, and when she rose to lead him to the fire, he followed, plumping down on the rug with a weary sigh.

Lars smiled. "King like it there. He get warm and rest his stiff old legs. He will join Old Tom, soon, I think. So, we make him happy now for short time."

Over a supper of mutton stew, thick with vegetables and dumplings, Gordon told the story of Old Tom and his rich strike. Molly's eyes grew big with wonder, and even Mother was a little excited.

"A gold mine! A real gold mine!" Molly exclaimed.

Lars chuckled. "It is more likely silver and lead we will be finding. That is what Tom look for."

"Oh, no, Lars," Molly insisted. "Gold. Hidden treasure is always gold."

"So? Then perhaps some little gold we will find mix in with the silver." The trapper's blue eyes were twinkling. "We must not let you have the disappointment."

"Well, anyway, you'll be rich, Lars," Molly said happily. "Just think—rich."

"But I do not wish for riches. Money, it do not bring contentment. No, when the mine is found, then half of it will be for you, Gordon."

"Half for me? Why? Tom left the claim to you."

"Tom would have want it my way. I know that. He would have wish me to share with you because you will help with the needed work on the claim."

"But, Lars—"

"So. It is settled. Half for you. Half for me," Lars insisted. And to all Gordon's arguments he only shook his head, saying, "Half belong to you and Jean and Molly."

Gordon glanced across the table at his mother to see that her face was flushed and eager, her eyes alive with hope, and he knew that she was thinking, as he was, that perhaps now they could leave the ranch and go back to the East. Molly's excitement seemed to be fading as theirs grew. She looked from mother to brother with troubled eyes, clouded with her concern. He tried not to see her downdrawn brows and quivering lower lip, but he knew what they meant.

"Could we do that, Mother?" he asked. "Take half?"

"I think so, Gordy—if that's the way Lars wants it. If the ore is rich, as Tom's note said, then there would be enough for all of us. Would you work the claim, Lars? Gordy would help, of course. Molly and I can manage the summer work until haying season begins."

"No. We will find a buyer. What does this old trapper know about mining? Or Gordon? Besides, we have not the equipment. No, we will sell."

"I'll help with the work," Molly offered, fighting tears, "but—oh, I don't want to. Because, Gordy, if you and Mother get rich, you'll leave the ranch." The tears won, and she finished in a wail. "I like it here. I don't want to go away."

"Aw, Molly," Gordon said, feeling sorry for his twin, "it'll be ages before we can go."

"Gordon is right, little Molly," Lars consoled. "The mine, it is yet hiding from us behind four streams, a blaze, and many gulch. And when we do find claim, the ore may not be rich. If rich, then time will be needed for selling. It is not overnight we find buyer."

"All right," Molly said, smiling tearfully. "Then I'm just going to keep on loving every day we stay here in our valley."

Gordon was all for starting back to Tom's cabin the next day, but Lars laughed comfortably and said that they both had work to do in preparation for the winter. When all was done, then they would look for Tom's claim.

Reluctantly Lars rose from the fire and went to the door to inspect the weather. "Snow is quit," he announced. "Come, King, my friend. We go home now, and I will carry you in my arms because you are tired old dog. Thor will get us both home without my hand on the reins."

The sky was clear the next morning, and two warm and cloudless days followed, with the hot midday sunshine ripping the new snows from the valley and the lower hills. Gordon decided to leave the cattle on the range as long as the forage remained uncovered, since delay would give him time to tackle the task of mending the break in the barn roof.

"There are a few shingles stacked in the shed," he told his mother. "The ones left over from the house roof. But there aren't enough to cover that big hole. I'll have to roof with brush and mud, I guess."

Molly's eyes danced. "I know where there's a piece of tin big enough to patch that hole. If you'll let me go along, I'll tell you how to find it."

"Of course you can go. I was going to ask you to help with the roof anyway. Where's the tin?"

"Up on one of those old fallen-down buildings in Sawtooth City. I rode up there with Father once, and he said, 'That tin will make a good roof when we need it.' There's lots there. It'll be fun going to Sawtooth City. May I go with Gordy, Mother?"

Once a lively mining town a few miles up the valley, Sawtooth City had been deserted since 1890, its log buildings crumbling into ruin. The valley people had helped along the inevitable destruction of wind and rain and snow, for whenever they needed boards or nails or beams, they simply took what they wanted.

"Would it be like stealing, Mother?" Gordon asked.

"Pfoo," Molly exclaimed in disgust. "Who's going to need anything there—except the ghosts, maybe?"

"Molly's right, Gordy," Jean Stevens said, smiling. "Ghosts have no need for roofs, and what is useful should be for the living." She began picking up the dishes quickly. "We'll all go. Gordy, you go hitch up Bonny and Camp to the wagon and put on the hayrack so that there'll be room for the tin. Molly, you do the dishes while I pack a lunch. Goodness knows, we ought to have a little pleasure before winter sets in."

As they drove out of the ranch gate, Gordon touched the whip to the flanks of Bonny and Camp, and they looked around reproachfully but increased their speed very little.

"They've been having it easy too long," Gordon said. "Oh, well, the hunting trip and today ought to tell them it's time to work."

Molly had been reading Sir Walter Scott when the ill-matched team had been bought, and had at once renamed them Campbell and Bonny. Camp was a big, long-legged gray gelding, alert to everything above his head, beneath his hoofs, and on each side. Bonny was chestnut, broad in the rump and short, and she plodded through her world in stupid half-sleep. Although she was Camp's half sister, she had little of his sense, managing to do her share merely by imitating her brother.

Gordon turned the horses from the road into a rough, disused trail that ambled off through the sagebrush. Letting the team slow to a walk, he began dreaming of money from the claim, of the changes that might come if the ore proved rich. He glanced up at the stately peaks and felt contented because someday he might be leaving them. When they drove through an aspen grove, the gusty October wind swept down on a gully full of brown autumn leaves to send them dancing across the trail in front of the team. Camp snorted, shied skittishly, and then settled sensibly to pulling the wagon again.

"Watch Bonny now," Molly said, giggling. "She'll wake up and spook in a minute."

Sedately Bonny poked on, sleepy head down. But when the fact that Camp had been frightened penetrated her thick skull, she tossed her head until the harness jangled, kicked up her heels, and shied violently. Camp glared at his silly sister, who looked foolish and then settled down to work.

The riders in the wagon laughed, and Mother said, "There's something very real and warm about Camp and Bonny. I think they love each other like human brother and sister."

Molly gave a small snort, another giggle. "That's right. Camp treats Bonny just the way Gordon does me—sort of patronizing. I'm just a girl, so I can't do all the things he does."

"You're certainly not like Bonny, dumb and slow," Gordon retorted. "Catch you waiting to follow my lead. You're always two jumps ahead of me."

Mollified by what she took for praise, she said firmly, "Well, anyway, I'm never going to let you give up Camp and Bonny. If we have to go back to the East, I'm going to drive them all the way and keep them ours. I love Camp for being so smart and Bonny because she's such a fool."

It was noon before the horses had pulled up the timbered ascent and through a canyon to reach the benchlike flat on which the mining town had been built. Gordon stopped the

team in the center of what had once been the main street and sat gazing around in silence at this place that had once been full of laughter and living. The sod roofs of the straggling cabins had fallen in from the weight of winter snows, but the log walls were still sturdy, weathered dove-gray by wind and rain and sun. Doors hung crazily on broken leather hinges; windows were staring vacant eyes, veiled sometimes by yellowed lace curtains. In the middle of the street a flagpole leaned flagless. Weeds, brown and dry, clattered and clashed in the patches that once were gardens. The sun shone, warm and golden on the forgotten homes, and the

crests of the great peaks rose serenely above the long ridges as if to say: "Man goes. We stay. We are mighty, but man is pigmy weak."

Gordon was aware of a sudden lost and lonely feeling, and he saw his mother shiver slightly. Even Molly was impressed.

"Brrr," she said after a long minute of silence. "I'll bet the ghosts come out at night and walk up and down the streets and in out of the cabins."

In spite of his own response to the eeriness of the place, Gordon didn't want Molly getting gloomy ideas, and so he jumped down from the wagon, tied the team to a hitching post still standing, and helped his mother to the ground. "Let's go find that tin," he suggested.

Molly climbed over the wheel and darted toward one of the largest buildings, calling back over her shoulder, "See, here it is, Gordy."

Most of the cabins had been roofed with boards, but he could see corrugated iron roofing on what must have been stores or saloons. Molly was tugging at a piece that had been ripped off by some gust of winter wind and had fallen half under a covered walk that led to an outbuilding. He went to help her, and they dragged the tin to the wagon, all three pushing and shoving the ungainly sheet up onto the hayrack.

"There," Molly said, ghosts forgotten. "Now let's explore."

For an hour they scrambled through the dilapidated cabins, stepping over the litter on the floors and pulling the flour sack linings from the walls to read the old newspapers tacked beneath for warmth. Although most of the useful objects had long ago been taken by the valley people, some of the cabins still held furniture—broken chairs and sagging bedsprings and rickety tables, hand-hewn. Rummaging about on cupboard shelves, Gordon found a coffee can full of nails, an old hammer head, and a pair of rusty spurs. Mother appropriated a faded painting, left hanging askew on a wall, and a mantel clock that actually ticked when she wound it.

Molly, who had wandered off outside, came running in, dragging behind her a carved and painted sign, once probably bright green, but weathered now to turquoise, its red lettering faded to a soft and lovely rose.

"What do you suppose it says, Gordy?" she asked, flushed and excited over her find.

"It's Chinese, I guess. Fred Curley told me there used to be lots of Chinese in here." Gordon chuckled. "Probably it says somebody would do laundry cheap. I tell you, Molly, we'll take it home and put it up over the gate, and then you can take in washing."

"Here, hold it, Gordy," Molly exclaimed. "I see something."

Down on her knees she plopped to grub around on a closet floor, backing out with treasure. "Look, Mother, it's pretty. What is it?"

"A button," Mother said, examining the square of red-brown stone. "No, it's somebody's locket. See, here's a loop of gold in the setting to hold a ribbon or a chain. And the stone has a face cut into it. Some woman prized this."

"It was a girl, I think," Molly said, her face serious. "A little girl. And she didn't mean to leave it behind. She looked and looked for it the last minute, with her folks waiting outside to drive off. Oh, how could they go and leave their home?"

Gordon saw trouble coming and hurried to say, "I suppose the ore gave out, and they had to move on to another diggings."

"It's strange to think of all the people who once lived here," his mother remarked dreamily. "Once it was a town of three thousand souls. All gone now, and their lonely homes seem to be calling them to come back."

Molly looked reproachfully at them, and her chin quivered. "That's just what you and Gordy want to do, Mother. You want to go off and leave our home lonely without us. And maybe—someday—strangers would come and find precious things we'd had to leave behind, and—"

Mother smiled her sympathy and tried to stop the threatened tears by saying, "Molly, dear, you've too much imagination. Don't fret until you have to."

But Gordon put his arm around his twin and hugged her close. "Never mind, Molly. It will be a long time before we can leave the ranch—if we ever can. Come on, let's eat. I'm hungry."

Mother set out sandwiches and cookies and milk on the sunny step of an old saloon, protected by cabins from the chilly October wind, and as soon as they had eaten, she wanted to start for home. But Gordon, with Molly backing him, insisted on taking the time to load a pile of boards torn from a frame cabin and some log timbers wrenched from a porch roof.

"I can use these for patching things up around the barn," Gordon said practically as they drove off through the sagebrush.

The next morning Gordon and Molly went to work on the barn roof, first mending the rafters with the timbers brought from Sawtooth City. Then Gordon fastened a rope around the tin and, tying an end of rope around his waist, climbed the ladder and clambered up to sit on the rooftree.

"Get out from under there before I pull up the tin," he called down to Molly. "Wind's coming from every which way this morning. It might catch under the tin and bang it against you."

With the roofing in place, he asked her to hand him up nails and hammer, and while he was kneeling at the edge of the low roof to reach down for them, a horse and rider came into the barnyard.

"It's Fred Curley," Molly said, and called out, "Hi, Fred."

Thrusting the can of nails into Gordon's hands, she ran to greet their neighbor. Fred was tall and gaunt, a narrow man with fading blue eyes, the skin at their corners crinkled with laughter lines.

"How are ye, Gordy, Molly," he called out. Fred was always noisily cheerful. "Where'd you pick up the tin? Been lookin' for a piece like that for me. Hey, boy, watch out—"

A blast of strong wind swooped down from the mountains to catch under the loose edge of the roofing and tilt it high into the air. Gordon reached for the tin as it sailed past him, but his balance was insecure. Nails showering about him, he plunged downward, landing on his side. When he rolled to sit upright, he saw that blood was running down his leg. He had hit on the tin roofing, and one of the rusty nails had been upright, waiting to gouge.

"You hurt, son?" Fred asked, dismounting and hurrying to help.

"Looks like I snagged myself. See, it's almost to the bone."

"Oh, Gordy!" Molly wailed, her face white. Brave as she was, she could not endure the sight of blood.

"Girls! Always getting sick over nothing," Gordon muttered crossly to Fred, for pain from the nail gouge was beginning to bother him. "Molly, you go on up to the house and bring me the turpentine and something for a bandage. And don't tell Mother what you want it for. We'd better not let her see this till it stops bleeding."

"Gosh a'mighty, Gordy, that cut ain't nothin' to get in a tizzy about," Fred said, his leathery face cracked into a broad grin. "Where's your axle grease? Ain't nothin' better'n axle grease to draw up a snag."

"Never mind, Fred," Gordon called after his neighbor, who, still talking, was energetically hunting the axle grease in the barn. "Molly'll be back in a minute with the turpentine."

"Here's the grease. Gettin' low, ain't ye, but there's enough to fix up that leg. Here, unwind your handkerchief and let me slap a wad of this on."

Gordon did not want the slimy grease on his leg, but Fred was not to be stopped. Talking all the while about its merits, he swabbed on a thick layer of the clammy brown stuff. To Gordon's surprise, the bleeding stopped.

"See?" Fred rattled on. "Only thing I know that's better is Sheepherder's Delight—that's alcohol and strick-nine mixed up with a little prune juice. Of course, it's made to take inside a man, and she stings some rubbed on outside, but the bite does the work. I fed some to an old prospector once—inside, of course—and he run right off and stole his own pack and hid it from himself in a bunch of willows. Powerful stuff, Sheepherder's Delight."

Fred threw back his head and laughed so hard at his own tale that Gordon could see the strong teeth, yellowed by tobacco. "Sagebrush wit," his father had always called Fred's type of humor, "because you can't choke it off before the next crop bobbles down on you."

Gordon stood up to find that the leg was growing more painful. Molly came running with a big bottle and a piece of an old sheet, and she was disappointed not to have them used, but interested in Fred's defense of axle grease as a remedy.

"Come on up to the house, Fred," she suggested. "Mother wants you to stay for supper."

"Nope. Got to be gettin' back. Sue, she's mighty testy when she cooks up a meal and I ain't home to eat it. I just rode over to tell you there ain't goin' to be much chance to get mail out now until spring. Banty Clagg, he came across the mountain road yesterday, and there's two feet of snow on the summit. This wind means rain, and rain this time of year is bound to turn to snow. Yep, she's a-settlin' in, winter is."

Gordon glanced across the valley and up at the mountains. Black clouds were climbing above the peaks, and whirling snow was a milky mist over the summits. A drop of cold rain spattered on the tin roofing.

"I ought to finish getting this roof on if snow's coming," he said, glancing down at his torn and bloody trouser leg.

Fred squinted up at the clouds. "Snow there, all right. You hobble on up to the house, son, and I'll finish the roof for you. Sue can wait supper for once. She'll settle down to a walk when I tell her I was helpin' out here. Molly, girl, let's pick up the nails. And then you can climb up with me and sort of steady the tin, case the wind comes again."

Gordon limped to the cabin, feeling ashamed because he had been annoyed by Fred, his remedy, and his humor. Like all valley people, he and his wife were always quick to offer needed help. It was Sue who had come to stay a week one time when Mother was ill, and it was Fred who had brought his wagon and team to help with the haying.

"What happened?" his mother asked, meeting him at the door. "What did Molly want with a piece of sheet? Oh, Gordy, you're hurt! Let me see."

He did not want his mother to see how deeply the nail had gone into his leg and refused to let her take off the bandage Fred had tied over the axle grease. Let Fred's remedy work, Gordon thought. That would please Fred and make up for those mean feelings about his jokes and his cures.

The leg pained him all night, and it seemed worse in the morning. Although he wanted to stay in the house and be lazy, after one look from the west window at the mountains, cold and sullen under thick, low-hanging clouds, he told Molly to go saddle their horses. With a storm threatening, the cattle up on the range must be brought down to the meadows.

"I'll help Molly, Gordy," his mother offered. "You can't ride with that leg."

"Sure I can. The sore place is on the outside above where the stirrup will hit. If I don't keep rubbing it on something, the leg can't get any worse."

The injury did hurt. As Gordon limped to the barn, he shook his fist at the mountains. "You just sit there and wait," he muttered to himself. "Wait until you can do a little damage, and then you send down wind or snow."

A gray-cold early dusk closed down over the mesa before they succeeded in rounding up all the cattle. It seemed to Gordon, impatient from the pain of his throbbing leg, that the cows stubbornly had hidden their calves in gullies or clumps of trees, and after they began the drive to the ranch, the steers insisted on bellowing and breaking away from the herd. Although Molly did most of the hard riding, it was dark before they drove the cattle through the barnyard and down to the meadow shelters that Father had built to protect the range cattle somewhat from the winter weather.

"Never mind forking hay off the stacks," he told Molly. "They'll eat stubble for a week or two—if the snow holds off. Snow's coming though. I can smell it."

They milked by lantern light. By the time the barn work was finished, he knew that he was in for trouble from the nail wound in his leg. It was hot to his touch, and he felt feverish. Painfully he limped to the cabin. Although he tried to keep his mother from knowing how he felt, she saw his flushed face and insisted on removing the bandage.

"Gordy, what have you put on this leg?" she asked. "The flesh is all inflamed around the edges of this brown stuff. What is it?"

"It's axle grease," Molly explained. "Fred put it on, and

he said the bleeding stopped right away. Fred says there isn't anything better to draw up a cut."

"Axle grease, Gordy!" Mother exclaimed. "Out of that dirty can that's been sitting in the barn for months! You should have known better."

Wiping off the grease with distaste, she bathed the inflamed leg with hot water and soap and then poured turpentine over the cut. Gordon winced and begged her to leave him alone. After supper he went to bed feeling hot and ill.

The next morning, when he awoke after a restless night, the leg was swollen, the flesh around the wound red and angry looking. He managed to get down the ladder, stretching himself out near the fire on the cot that served as sofa. When he said he didn't feel like eating breakfast, his mother insisted on looking at the leg again, and then she took from the shelf the big book, *The Family Physician*, that was a part of mountain equipment. Lips tight, she read, closed the book, and set it back on the shelf.

"Molly," she said, sounding worried, "you'd better saddle Phoebe and ride for Lars. This thing is something I don't know how to handle. He'll know what to do. And tell him what the wound looks like so that he'll know what to bring."

White-faced and grim, she went about her work, glancing occasionally from the window as she watched for Molly and Lars. Gordon dozed by the fire, feeling dull and doped. He slept, and woke to pain, and slept again.

When Lars came, he looked at the angry flesh and shook his head. "It is not good. Axle grease have stop the bleeding, it is true. But it have close the wound too soon. Dirt from barn is now in there—dirt from grease too—and they have cause trouble. You have bad infection, Gordon. We must cut open the place and cleanse. You can be brave?"

"Sure. Go ahead. I can stand it if I've got to."

As Lars worked, Gordon gripped the iron legs of the cot with his hands and shut his eyes tightly to avoid watching the work of the sharp knife that Lars had taken from a leather case. Somehow Gordon managed to keep from crying out when Lars poured over the wound a brown liquid that bit and burned.

"That will fix him now, I think," Lars said, as he bandaged the leg. "But we must watch carefully for a few days. We do not want blood poisoning to come."

Gordon opened his eyes to see Lars smiling at him in approval.

"You are good patient," he said, nodding his head. "Never tell yourself you are a coward. Pain you can endure, and that is something."

VI

The fever went away in two days, and under the trapper's care, the leg began to heal, but Mother would
not let Gordon go back at once to doing the ranch
work, insisting that Molly could manage, with Lars helping. Gordon sat in an armchair at the west window near the
kitchen stove, working at the algebra problems that Lars
set him each day or reading over again a book from their
scanty store or struggling with the hated grammar in the
writing his mother assigned him. Tiring of lessons, he
watched the snow fall on mountain and hill and flat, for
November had brought snows deep and lasting. There was
a day when big flakes fell softly from leaden skies, a day
when the sun broke through scudding clouds for a few hours
only to be hidden by more piling dark clouds from the mountain summits, a day when the wind blew cold and steady,
driving hard pellets of crystal before it and tossing
scarves of snow in long streamers of white smoke from the
high peaks.

Watching the daily storms, Gordon grew restless and
discontented. He knew that it was difficult for Lars to come
each day to help Molly with the chores. There was Tom's
claim too, still undiscovered. With all this new snow bury-

ing the trail, they would never get up to the cabin—much less find the claim under this thick covering.

On the fifth day, when Lars made his daily examination of the leg, he remarked with satisfaction that it was healed.

"Good. Then I'm going out tomorrow," Gordon said happily. "It's time I get back to work."

"No, Gordy," his mother protested. "You must give the leg a chance to get entirely well. The infection might come back. Besides, you're not very strong yet—after all that fever."

"The leg is well, Jean," Lars said quietly. "Infection will not come again. There is no reason not to let Gordon work, but if it please you, we keep your boy in a little longer. It is true the fever have take his strength. A couple more days you can wait, Gordon. There is no hurry."

"But there is hurry, Lars," Gordon insisted impatiently. "You're forgetting Tom's claim. If the snow gets much deeper, we'll never get up there until spring."

"And you're forgetting the skis," Lars retorted. "Snow is now two feet deep on flat, more in drifts."

"Horses?" Gordon asked hopefully.

Lars laughed as if delighted. "Too hard for them. This morning I ride my skis over here to save my old horse. No, we must ski to Tom's cabin now."

Gordon was dismayed. Now he'd have to learn to ski whether he wanted to or not, and he'd have to be good on skis to get up and down that steep trail.

"Lars, you're a mean old schemer," he said. "You're glad the snows have come. You knew I didn't much want to learn to ski."

"Well, I want to learn," Molly put in. "I think it would be wonderful."

"We will teach you both. And Gordon, finding Tom's claim will make reason for you to work hard at learning.

You will have to know easy way to keep going on flat. You will have to get uphill to Tom's cabin—get back down steep hill. All kinds of ski we will teach you."

Mother had been listening, and now she asked: "Lars, you aren't going to make Gordon go down big hills, are you? He might fall and break a leg or—"

"Big hill, little hill—all have same for boy who know how to ski, Jean. And now I think we better take look at those skis of yours, Gordon—Molly's also. And yours, Jean. Eleven feet on the flat out there I have seen the snow. So, we must all have means of getting around on top. Even you, Jean."

Lars and Molly went to the barn to hunt the family skis, which had been stored on the crossbeams, and Gordon was glad when they brought them into the house for his inspection. He was bored with staying in, eager for amusement. Lars provided the amusement. His tanned face set in lines of disgust, he angled the two pairs of long and awkward skis through the cabin door. Molly followed with her own smaller pair.

"Look at these stiff boards," Lars muttered as he set them up in a display row against the log walls. "Is it these you have call skis? No wonder you could not learn. Nobody could ski on these. This pair is not bad—have a little limber in them."

"That's Mother's pair," Molly explained. "Father took a lot of pains with them to make them real good."

"For you, Jean, these will do for little time because you will not be skiing as much as these young ones. Later I make you good pair. But look at these. Points almost flat. Get stuck in snow when any fool try riding them. Stiff, like iron. Heavy, like log. And all of twelve feet long."

"They're mine," Gordon confessed, laughing at the trapper's tirade. "I guess the points don't turn up because I was in a hurry to try them before Father had the points set right. Molly and I sneaked ours out of the frame he'd made. I remember Father scolded us."

"Lars, I wish you wouldn't teach them," Mother said. "Jim learned. And look what happened to him—skiing. If a snowslide should take Gordy too—"

Lars only looked stubborn, and Jean Stevens turned away, her face still and closed. Gordon knew that she was thinking of the splintered skis fastened to the still feet under the snowslide. No wonder she didn't want Molly and him to learn to ski. He'd take it mighty easy, he decided. No big hills for him. No prowling around in the mountains, where the slides could come roaring down with every thaw.

To Lars he said, a little belligerently: "What's the matter with my skis for length and weight? Everybody here in the valley makes skis like this. Fred Curley loaned us a pair for pattern."

"Because others do is no reason for making bad skis. I know better way. See, these skis are pine, heavy wood. Lift them. Too thick. Too heavy. Light ski ride on snow better than this heavy one, and a little shorter ski turn easier."

"These are mine," Molly put in, a gleam in her eyes. "Not much good, are they?"

"No good at all. We make new skis for both of you. At home I have seasoned boards of mountain fir—strong, light. Tonight I cut good length. Tomorrow we will make skis here. And for pole? What do you use for pole?"

"Well, each of us had a long heavy stick for balancing," Molly said. "I never used mine much. I went down good and fast without one, and when I went too fast—well, I just sat down."

"Long stick, heavy stick—no good. And only one! We make two pole for all of you."

"Two?" Gordon asked, puzzled. "What do we need two for? Nobody here in the valley uses two poles."

"I know that. In my own country men also use one pole. But I have ski much since I came here, and always I study how to do better. One pole a skier can use for balance. He can turn where he wish to go by putting pole into snow at side and leaning. He stop or slow down by sitting on pole between legs. But he cannot use one pole as way of getting fast over snow on flat."

"One's good enough for me," Gordon insisted stubbornly.

"I want two," Molly put in enthusiastically. "Anything to help me go faster."

"Two pole work better," Lars said. "Give skier arms to work with. It is like swimming. Nobody swim with legs only. He use arms too. Two poles let arms do part of work. We make two."

"But how can you stop?" Gordon persisted. "You can't sit on two poles at once."

Lars chuckled. "You could, but I know better way to stop. I will show you. But first we make skis and poles. Tomorrow I bring mountain ash for poles. Ash do not grow here in valley, but I have found some in canyon. I bring for all three of you."

When he came to the ranch the next day, he pulled behind him his small toboggan, loaded with two sets of boards and three pairs of poles. Smoothly planed to the right thickness, the boards were nine feet long for Gordon's skis, seven for Molly's. Thicker in the middle, each was thinned at the ends and each had a beautifully shaped point.

"What do we do with them now?" Gordon asked. "Father put the points in hot water to soften them so that he could turn them up."

"Better we steam them. Jean, have you big kettle which make lot of steam?"

She brought out the big copper wash boiler, and Lars filled it while Gordon built up a hot fire. By the time the barn work was finished and Molly and Lars back in the kitchen, steam was rising from the boiler. Rummaging in the lean-to, Gordon found some baling wire and brought it to the kitchen. He cut the wire in four lengths.

"Here, Molly," he said, "you climb up on a chair and run the ends of these wires over the rafters above the stove. Then we'll fasten the other ends around the skis and hang the points right in the steam."

Lars praised the idea, and Gordon began to be interested in making the skis although his mother asked crossly, "How do you think I'm going to get us a dinner? I can't crawl over this forest of boards. It's worse than wash day. You'll get a cold bite this noon, with no stove room for cooking."

The water boiled, the steam rose, and the room grew so warm that they had to open doors and windows. They ate the cold lunch while the points steamed, and then Lars and Gordon worked on the poles, with Molly insisting on helping. From the barn Lars had brought with him odd pieces of harness leather and strips of buckskin; the latter he soaked first in hot water and then wound in five places around the slender poles of mountain ash.

"When it dry," he explained, "it will tighten on pole. Make good and strong. We wind some around the top of each to make handle also, and now we fasten strips of harness leather under handle to make loop to go over hand. So. Pole will not get lost."

When the leather work was finished, he took flexible willow stems that he had brought and bent them into a circle ten inches in diameter, fastening the ends together with more rawhide.

"What are those things for?" Molly asked.

"Wait and you will see." He showed them a piece of old steel from a wagon tire. "I find this in your barn. I will take home and in my forge make a point for each pole. Then they will go easy into snow. I will soak the ends of these poles in water, and wood will swell and cause iron to fit tight."

"But what about the rings?" Molly persisted.

"The rings I will fasten to the pole above iron point with lacing of rawhide between circle and pole. They keep pole from sinking deep in snow, and you can push to make you go faster, Molly."

"You're wonderful, Lars," she exclaimed admiringly. "Just give you any old piece of scrap iron and some rawhide, and you can make anything."

"When we live in mountains, we must learn to use what we have," Lars said.

He made a wooden frame, large enough to hold the four skis. Setting them behind the bottom board of the frames, he let the points rest in front of the top board, nailing another one across at the place where they started their bend. "To fix points," he said. He ran a thin slat beneath the middle of the skis, nailing it firmly on each side of the frame.

"Now," he told Gordon, "you and Molly must not take the skis out of the rack until twenty-four hours have gone by."

"Then we can start learning to ski tomorrow when you come, Lars. May we?"

"No, no. You have too much of hurry, Molly. Still is much work to do on skis. We must smooth them down so that they will slip easy on snow, and we must make a device to hold foot to ski."

"That's easy," Gordon offered. "We'll just put a toe strap on them, the way Father did."

"I know better way. We make iron piece to hold toe of boot and something to hold heel for going downhill. You have boots?"

Molly ran to hunt two pairs of work shoes, laced well above the ankle.

"Hard toes, tough soles," Lars approved. "These will do. Now I go home to finish poles and make bindings. Tomorrow I do not come. Old King, he is not well. I stay home with him—work on bindings. Tomorrow, Gordon, you can go out to work. Get strength back. When I come again, we finish skis. Then—we learn."

Molly could scarcely wait until learning time came, and all that first day she caressed the skis in their rack and talked of flying down the hills. When Gordon thought of the steep pitches and the building speed of skis, he wasn't certain that learning was going to be fun. But he did as Lars had suggested—worked about the barn, snowshoed down to the meadow to pitch hay from the stack and scatter it over the snow for the cattle. Shaky at first, he found that strength came back rapidly with exercise.

Lars did not return until the fourth day. Over his shoulder he carried the finished poles, and the two sets of boots held tightly in the iron toe clamps bobbled at the end of rawhide thongs thrown about his neck.

"King?" Gordon asked. "Is he all right?"

"King is—all right. He have gone to join Old Tom. Last night. That is why I have not come before."

Molly cried, but Gordon, to hide his own distress over King's death, asked, "What are those shoelike things over our boots?"

Lars chuckled. "They are sort of—house for boot. See, I make them out of heavy canvas belting and fasten with flat screws to skis. They will help hold boot in place."

He inspected the skis and said the points were beautifully turned. Taking pieces of sandpaper from his pocket, he set them all to smoothing the running surfaces of the skis.

"Mine are all slick and slidy now," Molly insisted after a time. "Let's put them on and go try them out right now. Can't we, Lars?"

Lars shook his head and went on screwing the housings into place. He made rawhide toestraps to re-enforce the iron toeholds. Then with screws he fastened a hook on each ski behind the boot and ran narrow strips of strong leather through the eye and up over the instep of each boot, fastening the straps with a brass harness buckle.

"So," he said. "Buckle will make it easy to unfasten ankle strap for skiing on level or uphill, when heel need play. Fasten easy to go downhill."

"What's the good of all that?" Gordon asked. And Mother said, objecting, "If they fall, Lars, with the foot held as tight as all that, they'll break their ankles."

Lars was stubborn. "They will ski better with boot held to ski. We fix them this way. Next we must dope the bottoms so that they will run easy and fast on snow."

"Can't we just rub on a little of that stuff Mother uses to seal jelly glasses?" Gordon asked.

"No. My dope is better. I make it out of beeswax and pine resin melted with a cylinder from my Gramophone, which have broken. It is good dope—go fast downhill, not slip when go uphill. We put on now."

Gordon and Molly were impatient, eager to try out the new skis, but Lars serenely insisted on spending the rest of the afternoon and part of the evening putting layers of his dope on skis warmed before the fire. As a final touch, he painted the tops with varnish from a can he had brought.

"So. Snow will slide off top and water will not get into

the grain to warp the wood," he explained, setting the shining new skis up against a wall to dry the varnish. "Tomorrow we try them. You will come out too, Jean. I have dope for your skis also."

She came to run an exploring finger up and down the slick running surfaces of her old skis. "They'll go too fast for me. I'm glad you didn't put those boot binders and ankle straps on mine, Lars. I don't like them—for me, or for the children. They'll hurt themselves. There's danger in snow."

"Aw, Mother," Molly exclaimed. "What's there to be scared of? Snow's soft. It doesn't hurt you if you fall. It's like landing in feathers."

Several times that evening after Lars had left, Gordon ran a finger over the bottoms of his skis, remembering what his mother had said, thinking how fast the running surfaces would slide down the hills. He wanted to learn, he told himself. He had to learn or he couldn't help with the trapping. What was more important, he couldn't get up and down that steep trail to Tom's cabin—and he had to find the claim which was half his now. He'd learn all right, and do his best at the skiing, but he hoped that Lars wasn't going to make him run any of the really steep slopes. After he had gone to bed, he lay long awake, thinking with dread of the swift flight of skis flashing down. He slept at last to dream that he stood at the top of a great vast of down-dropping snow. Lars, grinning evilly, pushed him over the edge. Mother screamed and reached out a hand to stop him, but down, down, down swept his skis, and his legs shook under him. Ahead rose a great wall of icy rock. He tried to stop, but his skis took him willfully nearer and nearer. With a muffled moan he woke just as the rock rushed upon him.

"Whew," he muttered to himself. "What's the fun in that?"

However, he was ready the next morning, even eager for lessons to begin, when Lars came skiing smoothly over the flat. The sun was high over the eastern ridges when they all fastened on the skis outside the door. Gordon glanced at his mother, and she smiled shakily. He knew that she did not want to learn this skiing, but she was sensible enough to realize that it might be the only means of getting over the snow in case of accident or sickness for any of them.

"Now, we start," Lars said. "No. No, Gordon, Molly. Do not walk around like that with legs stiff. Keep knees bent. Now push right pole forward from shoulder and stick in snow with pole sloping backward. At same time push opposite ski forward. Now glide. Other side same. See, is easy."

Soon all three had begun to catch a little of the feel of the rhythmic motion, the co-ordination of pole and ski and body movement. Lars taught them to lean forward slightly, to keep the forward knee well bent, to straighten the arm at the end of each pole push.

"Blamed if it isn't fun this way, Lars," Gordon said. "Not hard work at all. What we used to do was just walking, not skiing."

"It's fun enough," Molly agreed, "but it would be more fun if we could slide fast down a hill. Can't we climb up and slide down pretty soon, Lars?"

"Climbing wouldn't be fun for me," Mother said, struggling up in discouragement from one of her many falls. "I've had enough. I'm going in to start dinner."

After the meal Lars took Molly and Gordon to a hill behind the ranch and taught them how to keep their skis in front of them as they climbed, how to press down the upper ski as soon as its glide stopped to keep from backward slip. When the slope grew steep, he set them to traversing back and forth across it.

"Glory!" Molly exclaimed. "Just think—we always used to take off our skis and walk up the hills, wading to our waists."

"Seems kind of silly now, doesn't it?" Gordon responded, for he also was feeling superior, proud of his new skill. But when they reached the top of the hill and he looked down the slope, his confidence left him.

"Fasten your ankle straps now," Lars ordered.

"This snow is pretty soft and deep, Lars," Gordon protested. "Maybe we ought to kind of pat down a smooth place before we start skiing."

Lars was scornful. "Deep snow is fun. And do you think you can stop to make smooth place every hill you come to on way from Tom's claim? No. You must learn to ski deep snow."

"But how? I always get a whole snowdrift between my knees. It trips me and I fall."

"I tell you how. When snow get deep and soft, then put your weight just behind toe irons. When you get to moving fast, let weight back to center of foot. That way the points of your skis come up a little out of snow. Watch and I show you."

Skis flat and close together, Lars slid down the slope, powder snow flying knee-deep behind him, but not building in front of his skis. At the bottom of the hill, he dropped his left knee low, thrust his right ski forward, and stopped in a long curving arc.

"See," he called up the hill. "Is easy. Like floating in snow."

"I'll float all right—up to my ears," Gordon muttered.

Molly giggled and said, "Me, too." Then she called down to Lars, "How did you turn like that? And stop?"

Lars climbed patiently back up the hill. "That is telemark," he explained. "It is way skiers in my country and in Norway stop and turn. I teach you."

Gordon practiced the telemark until he could do a poor imitation of what Lars did so easily, but Molly, tired of working, began sliding fast down the hill to fall in a flounder at the bottom.

"Pfoo," she said, blowing out snow. "What's the use of stopping and turning? I can stop all right—in a snowbank."

"Comes time," Lars said, "when turn is necessity. Maybe big rock coming up. Maybe tree. You must learn to stop and turn, Molly."

He showed them another way to turn, one that he said he had stumbled on one day when there was no time for the slow telemark.

"When you wish to make turn," he told them, "put weight on ski that is downhill. Upper ski will come around. Keep weight forward. Then when you come out of turn, put weight back so that skis will climb up out of snow. I show you. Then you try it, Gordon."

Gordon tried, but his skis crossed, and he dived head foremost into the snow.

"Fall sideways, if you must," Lars instructed. "Less danger of hurt that way. But maybe you not fall, if you use shoulders to help you swing around. I show you."

He kept them working until Gordon felt all his muscles aching with weariness and Molly's flushed face showed her exhaustion.

"We stop for today," Lars ordered. "You will learn, because every day we will practice. Is easy to teach you since you already know how to get around on skis. Not like start at beginning."

"Molly gets it faster than I do," Gordon muttered in discouragement. "I spend half my time in a snowdrift."

"Molly learns fast, yes. But you will be better skier,

Gordon, stronger skier. Molly likes to go fast too much to bother with doing exactly right."

Gordon saw his sister's chin firm with determination. "Pfoo," she muttered. "Gordy may be stronger because he's a boy, but I'll bet I get it right too."

Lars smiled at both of them. "The two of you stick to learning, and maybe soon you are boss of skis. We work a little every day. Now we go in for my hot coffee."

VII

*L*ars was a stern teacher, insisting that his pupils spend three or four hours a day gliding across the flat, climbing the hills, skiing down them. Mother early rebelled. Since she never meant to run the long slopes, she said, there was little use of her risking her limbs. She would come out to ski for half an hour on the flat or to slide fearfully, stiffly down the smallest incline she could find. Molly was showing a surprising gain in skill, perhaps because she yielded only occasionally now to her desire for speed without any controlling turns.

Gordon always worked seriously, for he had incentives. Before he could help run the trapline, before he could get to and from Tom's cabin to find the claim that was to bring wealth, he had to be master of the ungainly skis. Besides, he told himself, conquering his skis was the only way to beat the mountains and the snows they sent. And so he spent all the time he could spare from ranch work in practicing the technique that Lars taught him. He even rode his skis from house to barn and to and from the meadow where the cattle wintered. His leg and arm muscles grew so strong and hard that when he had to break the frozen snow with a mattock from the edge of the ditch and trample a wide path to let the cattle down to water, he found that the work was little effort for him. The daily skiing was building strength and endurance.

Thanksgiving Day came, with Lars sharing their dinner. Mother had sacrificed one of her precious hens as a change from venison. Baked golden brown, plump from its stuffing, the bird was placed on a platter encircled with a wreath of green pine sprays. There was stewed huckleberry sauce instead of cranberries, and there was mince pie made from venison and "pumpkin" pie from one of the big green squashes stored in the vegetable cellar. Mother had brought out the long white linen tablecloth that had been her mother's, the thin silver spoons with the wide bowls, and her treasured silver candlesticks.

As she lit the candles and their flames glowed softly in the late afternoon light, she said: "Once in a while we have to live like folks. Candles and white linen are necessities for the soul."

She asked Lars to say grace, and he bowed his head and spoke clearly: "Bless this food, God. Bless these kind people which have share with lonely old man. Bless this American day of Thanksgiving, which this man from far country is glad to have part in."

After dinner, with Mother and Molly clattering away at the great stack of dishes, Lars and Gordon sat by the fire to talk. Lars said that he must go the next day to the far end of his trapline, where he had a shelter stacked with food. He would stay there the night, he said, and ski back the next day.

"Am I good enough on skis now to go with you, Lars?" Gordon asked and held his breath as he waited for an answer. To run the trapline was the first step toward hunting the claim.

"I think so. You are stronger now, better with the skis. Yes, we will take you on this trip, which will not be so hard as getting to Tom's cabin. If this one you can do, then soon we go to find the mine."

Gordon was elated over both approval and permission, but his mother objected when she heard their planning. "Go off there in the snow for two days, Lars? Oh, no, Gordy, you mustn't. One of you might fall and get hurt. It might be you, Gordy. And then you'd freeze to death before Lars could bring help. I can't let you go."

While his mother and Lars argued, Gordon listened. Maybe, he thought, it would be better to stay at home from this trip and practice harder on his skis so that he'd be ready for the climb to Tom's cabin.

"If you'd rather I didn't go, Mother," he said, "I'll stay home."

Lars rose quietly and took his jacket and cap from a peg by the door. "If you do not wish to go, boy, I do not wish for your company."

Gordon felt the scorn in the quiet words. Was he staying home, he asked himself, just to please his mother? Or was he really unsure of being able to stand the long, hard skiing? Or could it be that he was alarmed at his mother's suggestion of the harm that might come to him?

"I think I'd better go, Mother," he said as firmly as he could. "I'll be all right. Nothing's going to happen, not with Lars along. What time do we start, Lars?"

The sun was over the eastern peaks the next morning when they set out from the ranch door. The snow squealed under Gordon's feet as he put on his skis and hunched into an empty pack in which to carry back pelts. Molly insisted on skiing a little of the way with them, and as they glided off across the flat Gordon could see his mother watching from the door. He had hated to leave when he saw the worry in her eyes, and now he almost turned back. But he waved instead and then dug his poles into the snow to catch up with Lars and Molly.

"Easy going today," Lars remarked. "That thaw we have last week have melt the snow. Now it is settled and packed down. And little fresh snow from yesterday make just right."

"It's so easy that I don't see why I can't ski the whole trip," Molly proposed. "I could do it. I'd promise not to get tired and slow you up."

"I wish you could come with us, Molly," Gordon said with regret. "But somebody has to stay with Mother."

Molly pouted, but did not protest, and Gordon smiled at her because he knew that, although she sometimes complained about her duties, she always ended up by doing willingly any task set her.

"It's cold," she remarked cheerfully. "You'll freeze your noses. Five below zero this morning."

"Be glad for us," Lars put in. "We will hope that sun will not drive away the cold. So. The crust will hold. If sun soften snow, going will get harder."

When they reached the river, Gordon told Molly that she must turn back. "If you get out of sight of the house, Mother will worry."

"All right for you, Mr. Bossy," Molly retorted, tossing back the pigtails that thrust themselves from under her red cap. "But you just wait. Someday I'll go, and you can stay home with Mother. I'll show you what a girl can do. See how fast I can go back."

At a swift pace she set off across the meadows, and Gordon smiled as he watched her, waving to her when she turned for a moment. For a girl, she really was good, and he was proud of her.

A few miles down the river Lars stopped where a hot spring kept the water free of slush ice. "We set trap for coyote here. Bounty bring ten dollars—if we catch. Coyote smart, hard to get. We set five trap here close to edge of bank under water. It take five trap to maybe catch one coyote."

Gordon watched while Lars set a trap in the shallow stream, fastening bait on a willow limb overhanging the spring.

"Here, give me a trap," Gordon said. "I'd better learn how to do this."

As they worked, Lars explained the habits of coyote. "Coyote, he is always hungry. Have big curiosity. So, to investigate he circle the bait, and to do that he have to get in water, but he don't smell trap because it is down in stream. Then, he step in trap, and we get him—maybe."

They moved on to examine the traps that Lars had set farther down the creek in a beaver pond, where the industrious little animals had dammed up a tributary creek to make their winter home.

"Is it true," Gordon asked, "that beaver can make a tree fall whatever way they want it?"

"No. Beaver cut trees that grow near banks of creek. Branches and limbs always lean toward water. So, when he cut tree, it naturally falls into water where he want it. Then he drag it to dam through water. Easy. They are busy little fellow—play as well as work. One time I see whole row of little ones slide down a slick log into pond. They keep crawling out to go back and slide again. Have a lot of fun."

Lars took two dead beavers from his traps, skinned the animals, and put the pelts in his pack before he reset the traps, planting them in shallow water near the shore. Each trap was fastened to a chain, which in turn was secured to a pole thrust into bottom sand. He peeled small willow twigs, dipped them in a bottle he took from his pocket, and fastened the twigs to the chains just above the water.

"What's that stuff?" Gordon asked, sniffing at the musky odor.

"Dope. I make from castor gland of beaver. He smell this dope, raise his nose toward it, and foot gets caught in trap. Sometime he drag chain to shore, but he can't get far away because chain get caught in willows. Beaver is smart. Sometime he spring trap with stick—even drag to dam and bury in mud."

"What do you do then?"

Lars chuckled. "Move on to another pond. Beaver in that one too smart for this old trapper."

They skied on to a line of high ridges in front of the eastern mountains, and Gordon asked, "What are we after now?" He was growing interested in this trapping business because it might be one way to make enough money to leave the ranch if his hopes for Tom's claim did not materialize.

"We trap marten here," Lars answered. "They live high on ridges. See, here are tracks in snow. He is elusive little fellow. You never see him unless you catch him—only his track."

The traps were set in trees all along the ridge, fastened loosely with nails to the trunks of pines, and Gordon noticed that the bait was so arranged that the marten would have to cross the trap to reach the lure. Lars had caught only one.

Gordon examined it with curiosity. "It looks like the weasels that keep robbing our henhouse."

"It is longer and pelt is a rich brown," Lars pointed out. "Marten fur bring good money. They travel far in winter to hunt mice and other small animal. They are—what you say—carnivorous."

For ten miles they followed the trapline until Gordon grew weary of the constant skiing. When the sun began to soften the snow on top, Lars insisted on breaking trail most of the time, but Gordon, wanting to do his share, occasionally pushed ahead. He tired quickly, however, and had to drop behind.

"Never mind," Lars said. "Skiing is making you stronger legs and lungs all the time. We are almost at my cabin now."

Late in the afternoon, when Gordon thought he could not push his skis into another stroke, they reached the shelter, which was no more than four unchinked walls and a dirt roof with a small trap door for entrance.

"I fix him this way," Lars explained, "because when snows get deep, it is easier to dig down to trap than to shovel out high door."

Inside there was a dirt floor, hard-packed, and a small rock fireplace for heating and cooking. A rough table made from a hand-hewn log slab and two three-legged stools provided the only furniture. From the dry wood piled to the ceiling on one side of the cabin, they soon had a fire blazing and crackling on the hearth. Lars lit a lantern and brought out an old tin coffeepot and a round Dutch oven of heavy black iron. Rummaging among the tightly tinned supplies, he found the makings for soda biscuits and mixed them, baking them in the Dutch oven buried in the coals of the fire. With canned beans, and bacon cut from the flitch that was suspended from the ceiling in a tin can with holes bored in the bottom for air, they made a good meal.

"Have to keep everything tight from those pesky packrat," Lars said. "Even the blankets. I roll them tight and hang from rafters with wire. Packrat he crawl down my wire, but then he come to these little round pieces of tin I string on wire. They teeter with him, let him down to floor again. He get discourage—some. Take a lot to discourage those little animal."

Gordon was glad to crawl under a blanket on a fir bough bed near the fire. Weary from the long skiing, he went to sleep instantly, but he wakened during the night to hear a roaring among the branches of the pine trees above the cabin.

"Golly," he muttered to himself, "hope that wind doesn't bring snow. Make it hard getting down."

When he woke in the morning to the light of the lantern, he noticed that a fine ridge of white had sifted between the logs. Lars, who was getting a breakfast of more bacon and biscuits, looked worried.

"It's snowing, isn't it, Lars?" Gordon asked. "Much?"

"Not bad. We go right after breakfast. It is best that we hurry down. The sky look like big storm come."

Gordon climbed the ladder to the trap door and peered out to see fine snow sifting through the branches of the pines. Out over the valley and above the peaks the clouds hung black and low, and although the wind had died down, the air felt dense and heavy. They hurried through breakfast, put food and blankets away, and climbed into their skis.

"We go back different way," Lars explained. "Shorter way. I make a circle with my trapline. We will ski as fast as we can, but we must take anything in traps and bait again."

Going down took less effort than the climb of the day before, but in the new soft snow the skiing was tricky, for the trapline led them between the ridges through canyons filled with fallen logs and rocks under the snow. Much of the way they had to sidestep, except in those places clear of brush and trees. Although stopping to bait the traps took time, Gordon was glad for the rests while Lars inspected his traps. There was a red fox in one.

"Red fox is good," he said, "but sometime I catch silver fox, and that is better."

Gordon had lost all interest in the animals trapped. "How much farther before we hit the flat?"

"Not far. But look down there."

Gordon saw that a dark cloud covered the entire valley. Fog! Skiing in that was going to be bewildering; he had heard of riders who had lost their way in fog and only reached home by giving horses their heads. His mother would be worrying, running to the door to watch and listen. Why had he ever come on this trapping jaunt anyway? His leg muscles ached from the constant checking and sidestepping, his arms from the continual poling.

Down, down, down they worked, taking almost as much time as they had in climbing the day before. In the whirling snow, driven now by a cold wind, they dared not slide on their skis in the narrow canyon. It was too difficult to see ahead, too hard to avoid the looming rocks and trees.

After what seemed like hours of scrambling downward, they found themselves inside the gray mass of cloud that had rolled from the peaks to conceal the valley floor. Gordon knew when they reached the flat only because his skis no longer tipped downward, but he could not see their tips, could not see the small pitches and rises of the not too level terrain. The wind had been left above the clouds, but inside the fog the snow seemed to come from above and all around, smothering him like a shower of feathers, blinding his eyes, getting in mouth and nose. Although it was still afternoon, he seemed to move in a twilight world where there was no shadow, no looming bulk of familiar boulder or tree.

He tried to keep to rhythmic gliding, but his skis sank in the soft snow, his poles found no grip. He struggled on, fighting the welter of white feathers beneath his skis, above him, around him, consoled by the knowledge that Lars was

just ahead, that all that was necessary was to follow in his tracks.

Tracks? What tracks? I'm skiing snow that's never been broken, he told himself in sudden panic. I'm off the trail. A fellow could get lost in no time in all this smother. Wander off. Never be found.

Trying to calm himself, he felt around in a circle with his skis to find the deep cuts that must have been left in the snow. Surely they were not far away. But there were no tracks. He was lost.

"Lars!" he shouted frantically. "Lars! Where are you?"

"Here. Just ahead and to the right. I wait for you."

Gordon skied in the direction of the calming voice until, out of the gray fog, the trapper's bulk loomed large and shadowy.

"I—I got off the track, Lars. I thought I was lost."

"It is easy to get lost away from each other in this cloud. We keep near together now. Let your skis feel the way, and follow me close."

"Go slowly, Lars, or I can't keep up with you. Do you know where we are? How can you find the way in this storm?"

"Do not be alarm. It will only make you work too hard, lose strength. Ski as easy as this snow will let you. We are in trouble, yes. But I will find the way. Just follow."

They pushed on slowly. Although Gordon's panic was over, he felt as if he swam in a gray ocean of fog and snow, glided in a world of gray. By concentrating, however, he found that he could easily follow the deep tracks because his skis slid more easily in them than in unbroken snow, but several times he missed the trail and had to feel about with skis and poles to find it again.

For hours, it seemed to him, he trudged on blindly, and then the high wind above cut down in a powerful gust to slice a rift in the cloud. Ahead he could see Lars, plodding steadily on as if he knew the way. Covered white with snow from his old blue cap to his skis, he looked a part of the storm, akin to it. If an old man like Lars could stand the hard skiing, Gordon told himself, then he, who was young and strong, could also keep going.

The wind died. The cloud settled down again. In spite of his weariness Gordon pushed on with vigor, aware of a new feeling growing within him. He lifted his head and faced the fog and the storm. Mentally he shook his fist at them. No old cloud, no snow, not even the mountains that sent the storm, could defeat him. Not while he had life and determination. He laughed at himself then for all those lofty thoughts. After all, the only thing he had to do was to stay in the tracks. Keep his tired body going. Not lose heart. It was Lars upon whom safety depended.

Put one ski in front of the other and push. Pole and push and glide. Pole and push and glide. Keep going. Keep going. Keep going.

The words in Gordon's mind became the rhythm of his skis as he slogged ahead, following the tracks that grew ever deeper in the soft new snow. He felt no surprise when a tiny point of golden light blossomed ahead. He was home. And he had known for the last half hour that he would get there. He slogged on toward the light that grew from pinprick to a square, blurred and misty through fog and drifting snow.

"We make it," Lars said, stooping to take off his skis.

Gordon saw the doorstep and fell down on it suddenly, sidewards, his skis held awkwardly out in front of him. His head bumped the door, and it opened to light and warmth.

VIII

December brought a long spell of bright and sunny weather, with nights below zero and days crisp and cold, except during the midday hours. The snow melted a little at noon, settled and packed, and the barometer stood at a steady high.

After a few days of this, Lars came skiing over from his cabin one afternoon. "Better we go up to Tom's place now, Gordon. We try again to find his claim. I think these sunny days will hold. Tomorrow we go."

"Good," Gordon said, scarcely able to contain his delight. He had been working and waiting a long time for this.

"Skiing will not be easy," Lars warned. "Lots of climb."

Gordon only laughed. "After that trapping jaunt with you, I'm ready for any old kind of skiing—or weather."

Early the next morning they poled off from the ranch, each carrying only a small pack containing extra dope for the skis, sandwiches for noon, gear for mending the bindings, and dry socks.

"Better we go light," Lars had said.

In dawn twilight they glided across the firm snow of the flat, the mountains looming above them, immense and clean and white against a dark blue sky. Gordon chuckled to himself, thinking that they two must look like small black bugs crawling across the vast, unbroken white of the plain. He was shivering a little from the bite of the early morning cold, but as his blood warmed from poling and pushing, he forgot the mountains and his own insignificance. He loosened his muffler and bent his strength into each stroke.

"Do not work too hard," Lars warned. "Long way we must ski. Save your strength for uphill."

When they entered the forest trail, the snow was so soft under the pines that they had to take turns breaking trail, stopping occasionally for a rest. At noon they came to the small meadow where they had seen the buck dancing on the golden grasses. Snow lay deep over the meadow now, but in the sun they found a fallen tree, split by lightning and still clinging to its trunk above the drifts. Brushing a cap of white away, they sat on the slanting thick boughs to eat their lunch, not even taking time to remove their skis.

It was dusk when they reached the familiar clearing with Tom's cabin standing forlorn and silent, almost buried under snow.

"No one have been here," Lars said, opening the door after they had shoveled it free of snow. "Everything is just as we left it."

Gordon sniffed the chill air. "Our friends have been here—the packrats. I can smell them."

"Is nothing," Lars said, chuckling. "We sweep out and clean up a little."

Soon they had a fire crackling in the old stove, warming the cold cabin to cheerfulness. Gordon broke ice on the creek to fill the waterpail and sawed steaks from the frozen venison haunch while Lars mixed biscuits. In a heavy iron kettle he put beans from Tom's supplies and shoved them to the back of the stove to soak.

"Cook all day tomorrow," he said. "Eat for supper."

They kept the fire going during the night in order to

have the cabin warm for sleeping, and in the early morning hours, as the heat mounted to the rafters, snow slid from the roof with a roar. The noise wakened Gordon, and reluctantly he crawled out of his blanket to stoke the fire. After he was back in his bed, he could not sleep. He thought of the wealth the claim might bring if they found and sold it and of taking his mother and Molly to the East. They would go back to their old home, to the little Ohio town with the quiet streets shaded by tall leaf trees. Of course, Molly might be unhappy at first, but he'd make it up to her in some way. He'd see that she had a good time, take her to parties and dances, and there would be school for both of them. She would soon forget the ranch. He might miss the mountains himself—a little—just at first, he decided, and was startled by that thought. But life here in this valley was too hard on his mother, who always used to be happy and gay. Now she was quiet and sad, and the ranch work was wearing her down to gauntness. He had to—

In the midst of all his planning of how he would spend the fortune he was going to make, he went to sleep.

The next morning they breakfasted on flapjacks and honey from the pail that Tom had stored for "winter sweetning," the valley term for syrup, jam, molasses, or honey. Lars shoved the beans to the front of the stove.

"We come in sometimes to get warm," he said, "and then we stoke the fire. So. Beans will cook."

They spread Tom's letter out on the kitchen table to freshen their memories about his directions.

"First thing to do is to find that blaze," Gordon said. "Then we can go on from there."

Lars sighed. "Two creeks. Remember? Blaze could be on either one."

"Then we'll just have to search both of them again. Come on. Let's start."

They began by working the creek that ran from west to east on the south side of the shack, examining every tree, but finding no blaze. The creek on the other side also yielded no sign of Tom's ax mark. The search was tiring because they had to wear their skis, since the snow was five feet deep in the clearing. Noon came, and they had found no sign of even the tiniest blaze chipped from a pine. Tired and hungry, they went into the cabin to eat a hasty lunch of warmed-over coffee and cold venison steak wrapped in the pancakes left from breakfast. Lars added plenty of water to the beans and slid the kettle to the hottest part of the stove.

"So," he said. "Tonight they will be ready."

"Look, Lars," Gordon said, when they started the search again, "I'm going to take off my skis and crawl under these firs that come way down to the ground. There isn't much snow under these thick branches. Maybe Tom hid his blaze low down there—just to make it hard for us."

Gordon floundered down the banks of snow to the drier spots under the firs. Lars joined him, and although they hunted for the rest of the afternoon, covering three or four feet back into the timber, they found nothing.

At dusk, legs and arms tired, faces scratched from branches and brush, cold and discouraged, they gave up the search. The cabin was warm, and the aroma of the cooking beans gave them appetite in spite of their dejection. After the meal was over, Gordon leaned his head on both hands and allowed himself to express what he was feeling.

"A whole day gone! And we're not one bit closer to that claim than when we started. What's wrong with us, Lars?"

The trapper smiled ruefully. "It look like we are—not smart. Or else Old Tom was too smart."

"Hey, wait," Gordon exclaimed, lifting his head as a sudden idea struck him. "Lars, wasn't there a big wind storm a few days before we came up here last fall?"

"Yes. Big storm. Some shakes blew off my roof, and I have to put him on again. So, I remember. Why?"

"Because maybe that wind blew down the tree that Tom had blazed. He might have been too ill to notice. That blaze might be out there buried under the snow, and that's why we couldn't find it."

Lars looked encouraged. "You make good use of your head, boy. Tomorrow we dig."

Armed with shovel and crowbar, they set out again the next morning to dig in the snow around the fallen trees and examine them. The ones too big to move with the crowbar, they undermined to inspect the trunks as far as possible. But they found no blazed tree. Late in the afternoon, disheartened, they stopped to rest. Gordon swept the snow from one of the stumps where Tom had cut down a tree for his clearing. Snow makes a cold perch, and he brushed off as much as he could. Suddenly he peered closer.

"Lars, look here!" he called in excitement. "What do you make of this mark?"

Scratched in the flat center of the stump was a crude arrow, the snow-filled lines standing out sharp and clear.

"It look like arrow."

"It is an arrow, Lars. And it's pointing east—just opposite the place we've been hunting the hardest. Do you suppose—? Could this be the blaze?"

Lars shook his head. "Not on tree by creek, which is what Tom say. Maybe this is just idle scratching one day when he sit down to rest. Maybe signal."

"Well, at least it points toward a creek—that one to the east. Come on, let's look over there."

For an hour they hunted, but there was no sign of a

blazed tree. Just at dusk, when Lars was talking of quitting the search, Gordon pulled a small broken tree out of his way in order to reach a larger one and was about to toss it to one side when he saw a fairly fresh ax mark on the sapling.

"Look, Lars, look!" he shouted. "I've found it. The blaze. Look here. Isn't that it?"

On the under side of the sapling was a tiny triangular cut, too small to be noticed by anyone not searching earnestly.

"It is blaze," Lars pronounced. "But this tree is no wind-fall. It has been cut down, and blaze was hidden underneath. That Tom! He have plenty cute. He chop down this tree on purpose to hide blaze. He want to make me work to find his riches."

"Well, anyway, let's go see if we can find the rest of the way to the claim. At least we know which creek to cross."

"No. Dark is come. We go in now. Eat more beans. To-morrow we hunt Tom's claim."

Gordon was silent all through the evening meal, for one fact bothered him greatly. Cutting down a tree to hide a blaze seemed mighty foolish.

"Lars, why should Old Tom go to such pains to hide his mark from us?" he asked finally. "It just doesn't make sense. He told you how to locate his strike, and then he tried to keep you from finding it."

"I know that. I have been wondering. I know it was not his friend that he try to confuse. I think—maybe he want to keep somebody else away."

"Somebody else? But who?"

"I do not know. But I am thinking that maybe when he find this rich ore, he write to—outsiders. Try to sell. Old Tom, he did not care about working a mine. Many times before this he have dug up wealth and sold his claim. He wish only for money to grubstake him while he hunt more strike."

"You mean somebody else knows about Tom's claim?" Gordon asked, aghast, and then grasping at any hope, he added, "But he hasn't been out of here to mail a letter since early this summer. We'd have seen him go by on his way to the store."

"I know. I come up here in August, and he had not found ore then or he would have say so. After that he make his strike. Maybe he get somebody else who come here to mail letter for him. Maybe go by after dark and not stop."

"I begin to see," Gordon said, "why he was so sly about that blaze. He knew he was ill, and you had told him he might die. His heart got worse. He'd sent off that letter and knew that these buyers might come to inspect his claim, but he wanted you to have it. And he had to leave directions so you could find it."

"That is right. Maybe last thing he did was put note in hollow tree and then fix blaze. If strangers come, they find him, maybe even find hollow tree. But not little tree cut down with his mark on under side. Old Tom was plenty smart."

"Golly, Lars, if somebody else knows he'd made a rich strike, then we've got to find that claim this time. We can't wait to come again."

Lars did not seem much concerned. "Tomorrow we find. We have the key now—the first step. Other steps will be easy. And do not worry, boy. No city man is going to come to this valley in all this snow. Not unless he want claim pretty bad."

Gordon scarcely slept, so eager was he to start the search anew. He hurried Lars through breakfast and out into the snow at dawn. They crossed the creek by the blazed tree and tried to walk the ten paces "strate ahed," as Tom had directed, but it was difficult to judge a pace on skis, impossible floundering on foot through the snow. In a small meadow, however, they found three boulders at the end of what seemed like ten paces to them.

"Now which of these boulders did Tom mean?" Gordon asked, exasperated at the vagueness of the old prospector's directions. "They're all big. It could be any one of the three."

"We try them all. And when we find small gulch beyond with down tree, then we have use right boulder for start."

On the second try they found the tree, a huge pine fallen across a deep gulch. Gordon wanted to ski over the snow-mounded log, but Lars said sensibly that it would be foolish.

"A broken leg up here would be—not smart. We not find Tom's diggings, and we stay here until leg mend. Can't ski down on broken leg."

They sidestepped down into the gulch and climbed the other side. At the other end of the pine bridge they turned sharply left to ski what they estimated must be about fifty-two paces. A few ski strokes beyond they found the second gulch with its creek singing under ice. Gordon was elated at first by their success, but his spirits plummeted suddenly down when he thought of Tom's indefinite instructions.

"How do we go on from here?" he asked in frustration. "Tom just said to work to the northeast, and he didn't say how far. Could be twenty miles to the northeast."

"Not that far," Lars said, laughing at Gordon's impatience. "Old Tom was lazy man. Read again what he say."

Gordon took the note from his pocket and read aloud. "It says: 'tunel hole in rock wall. stakes mark clame. I think ore is rich.' Well, maybe the ore is rich, but we're never going to find any old hole under all this snow. It will be drifted full. We could ski right on top of our mine and never know it."

"We just tramp around in all these boulders and keep going northeast. Maybe find hole. Maybe not."

All afternoon they hunted over the rocky hillsides to the northeast, discovering two or three holes, where Tom had evidently dug and found ore of no value. But there were no stakes and there was no marker, although they kicked around the holes with their skis and dug with their poles to find any short stake that might have been buried under snow.

"Let's go up this little canyon," Gordon suggested finally. "It leads sort of northeast."

They found more holes in the canyon, but no claim stake. Finally Gordon's sharp eyes saw a snow-covered mound at the distant head of the gully and skied rapidly toward it.

"Here's a stake, Lars," he called back in wild excitement. "It's sticking up out of the snow an inch or so. Hurry up here. I can't wait."

He took off a ski and standing on the other one began digging in frantic haste. And sure enough, there not far below the snow line was a tobacco can nailed to the stake! With fingers that trembled, he took off the tight lid and drew out a small slip of paper.

"We've found it, Lars! We've found our claim!" he called to Lars as the old trapper came skiing up to the mound.

"Read what Tom say."

Gordon unfolded the dirty paper and read the scrawled words aloud:

"notice is hereby given that Tom Rider has lokated ore here on october 5–1902. on this day i Tom Rider lay clame to a mining clame on this vane. 200 ft. northerly from this stake is red fir on first corner—blased. clame bears

e. 84 ft and w. 183 ft. red fir 25 inches in diam. blased
672 ft. southerly from this stake marks s. end of clame.
this lokation lays between Elk mounten and Kresus peak
to e. of Beaver crick."

The claim slip was signed *Tom Rider*.

"After all this hunting, we have it," Gordon exclaimed,
sighing his relief. "It's ours. It will make us rich."

"Maybe it make us a little money," Lars remarked
temperately as he prodded around the stake with his ski
pole. "There's a big hole here. Perhaps four feet wide.
See, it goes into canyon wall. This is Tom's tunnel, I think."

"I'm going to crawl in," Gordon said, hastily taking off
his other ski.

He scrambled down into the hole Lars had started, throwing out the snow behind him until he was on dry rock. "It's
sort of a cave," he called back through the opening. "About
ten feet long, I'd say. And there's lots of ore lying around."

He backed out with his pockets stuffed full of samples
of what looked like white quartz, dark-veined. Lars took a
piece, scratched at the dark spots, spat on them, and rubbed
—and they turned blood red.

"Ruby silver," he said. "I have hear Tom talk about it.
I have seen him do this to ore to tell what it is."

"There's a whole big vein of this stuff in there, Lars.
I lit a match to see. Maybe the vein runs deep, and it's
three feet wide on the surface. Golly, do you suppose the
ore is really rich?"

"My friend think so. But only an assayer can tell us for
sure. We must now get to the store in Stanley to see if
we can find any person which is going out of valley. We
will get him to mail our samples to assayer in Hailey. He
have office in that town. Maybe he will find lead in ore
also."

"What do we do now?" Gordon asked. "Change Tom's claim to our names?"

"Yes. You write, Gordon. You will put it better than I can."

"Let's give our mine a name, Lars. It ought to have a fancy name."

Lars smiled. "What would you like to call it?"

Gordon thought for a moment. "I know," he said. "Let's call it the Molly Mine. It sounds good, and Molly would be pleased. Maybe it will make up to her a little for what's going to happen if this claim brings in any money."

"You mean—leave the ranch? Move away from mountains?" The old trapper glanced down at the soiled and trampled snow, and when he looked up again, the disapproval had gone from his eyes. "Is good country here. Maybe you change mind. Anyway, it is good to name this claim for Molly. So. It is now the Molly Mine."

They wrote the name on the brown paper their lunch had been wrapped in, and then Gordon copied over Tom's phrasing, substituting their own names and correcting the spelling.

"Hadn't we better plant a small tree on top of the mound?" Gordon asked. "It would stay green in the snow and look as if it grew there. Then next time we come we can find the claim easily."

"No. Little tree all alone in canyon where no tree grow —that is foolish. Even city man would know tree not just grow on top of mound of snow."

"You think of everything, Lars," Gordon said. "We can't let anybody find this place."

"So. We will leave stake as it is with tobacco can and our claim inside. Deep snows will bury. Nobody else find, but we will know where it is." When they had restored the stake and smoothed over the dug snow, Lars said, "We will go home now—back to valley. Tomorrow—early."

Gordon was so happy that skiing down the narrow trail the next morning was fun. Although it had taken them a whole day to climb up, they were down on the flat in a short time. As they glided across it side by side, he asked Lars, "What's the next step after we get the assayer's report back?"

"If ore is rich, then in spring as soon as the pass is open, we drive over the mountain to file on claim. It is not ours until then."

"Golly, how can we wait that long?" Gordon exclaimed. "Couldn't we ski over?"

Lars shook his head. "To ski that steep mountain would be foolish—unless somebody in valley have real necessity."

"Well then—look, Lars, it's still early. Why can't we just ski on down to the store? Mail our samples now. When the report comes back, then we'll at least know if we have something in this claim of ours. We could stop at the ranch and tell Mother we were—"

"No," Lars interrupted, vetoing the plan firmly. "You are in too big hurry. I must run my traplines again, and you have promise to help. Besides, it is nearly Christmas, and on that day, like always, we go to the McCartys' house for big dinner. It is only five miles from there to store. Then we will mail samples. Do not worry. No city mining man will find our claim. For mountains and snow they would have big fear."

Gordon glanced up at the proud might of the peaks, glittering so clear and sharp in bright sunshine that they looked almost friendly. The claim was safe enough with them, for they would soon send storms to cover stake and can and trampled snow with fresh white. The mountains would keep the secret.

IX

*G*ordon knew that he would have to forget for a time his eagerness to find out about the samples of ore and turn his thoughts to the preparations for Christmas. His big problem was going to be to get his mother the six miles from the ranch to Fred Curley's place, from which the road had been broken open to the settlement. She was not strong enough to ski the distance, and he knew that he must break out his own section of road so that she could ride Phoebe as far as Fred's. From there, of course, they would all join the Curleys to go the rest of the way in a big wagon.

Two days before Christmas, with the mountains giving promise of a few days of clear weather, he went to the corral to hitch the team to the big sled runners. Camp was a good snow horse, and Bonny would work hard enough if she followed her brother's lead. But before Gordon reached the barn, he heard a high shrill yipping and saw Fred Curley driving his dog team through the ranch gate. The dogs were running fast, the leader far out in front, the others strung out in a long line of singles behind, with Fred shouting orders from his perch at the back of the sled. Swiftly it skimmed over the snow to come to a flourishing stop in front of the barn.

"How are you, son?" Fred shouted, his lean old face red from the wind of his speed. "Just came to tell you I'll drive over tomorrow about sunup with the dogs and cart your ma over to my place. Save you havin' to break road."

"That's kind of you, Fred," Gordon said. "I was just going to begin the job. Mother would love a ride behind your dog team. Molly and I can ski over so there won't be too much of a load, though I bet Molly would like to try flying behind the dogs. Me, too."

"Like a ride right now? You and Molly both. She's pretty light. Call her."

Gordon grinned. "No need to. Here she comes. Look at her run. She's afraid she'll miss going for a ride."

Molly came flying, her knit cap crookedly over one ear, only one arm in the jacket she was struggling to put on as she ran. "Oh, Fred," she called out, "give me a ride. Please. Please. Your dogs looked so pretty coming through the gate so fast. I just can't stand it if I don't get to ride behind them."

"He's going to take us both," Gordon told her. "Here, let me help you with that jacket. It's going to be cold, riding."

"I like this first dog," Molly exclaimed, reaching out a hand to pet him. "Can I touch him? What's his name?"

"Sure you can. He's got a real sweet disposition. That's old Mike, a tarnation good lead dog." Fred was off on his usual stream of talk and anecdote. "He knows all the orders —does all the guidin'. He can smell out a trail weeks after he's been over it once. Got a mind of his own, old Mike has. He saved my life one time when I tried to tell him to go over the edge of a canyon in a fog. Just turned up his nose at me and went the other way. Mike has got more sense than a human. Well, get in. Get in. Tuck up good in that fur robe. Right snappy this morning."

Molly and Gordon settled themselves on the hand-made sled, with its long handles behind, its sturdy frame laced with rawhide to form the seat. When Fred shouted, "Mush!" the dogs bent their strength into the collar bands, the belly bands tightened—and they were off. Built on a pair of skis, the sled skimmed lightly over the snow, with Fred running along beside at the start and then stepping up to his little platform behind the sled.

Gordon nudged Molly. "Look, no shafts. No reins. Just that rope down the center."

She nodded. "It's that nice lead dog that does the guiding. And Fred, of course."

Mike really did no actual work, they discovered; he never tightened a trace, never pulled, but he understood and obeyed Fred's orders and bossed the other dogs. Fred shouted, "Gee!" and Mike turned to the right, "Haw!" and he turned to the left.

"Watch that second dog from the rear," Molly said, giggling. "The little black one. He's trying to get out of work."

The little black dog looked around inquiringly and then reared back to throw himself on his side, but the other dogs unconcernedly dragged him along until his hide grew uncomfortably warm. Then he tried the other side. The end dog, a big tan and white part-collie with a stub tail, nipped at the hind quarters of the lazy one. The little black dog thought it over hastily and decided to get up on his feet, although he made them go only fast enough to keep a little ahead of his tormentor and certainly did no pulling with his shoulders.

"Watch Old Bobbie now—the collie," Fred shouted from the rear. "He's my wheel dog, next to the sled. That little Bimbo, he's new, and he's been pesticatin' around all the way over here. Watch Bobbie teach him to get into the collar and work."

The collie kept nipping at the hind quarters of little Bimbo, who had to move swiftly to keep ahead of the snapping teeth. Soon Bimbo was pulling his share.

Faster and faster the sled flew over the snow. The sun sparkled on the crystals of frost, and the range loomed white and still across the valley against a blue-bright sky. Gordon saw Molly's glance turn to the mountains and then back toward the ranch buildings, their logs warmed to golden brown by the morning sun.

"Doesn't it look homey and nice—with the mountains so big all around?" she said, and went on as if not expecting an answer. "It's fun living here too. Gordy, you'd never get a ride behind a dog team back East."

Gordon was relieved when Fred at that moment turned the dogs and they curved back toward the ranch. Molly was going to be a problem if those samples they were going to send in really proved to be rich.

"It's such fun, Fred," Molly called back. "Your dogs go fast."

Fred, of course, responded with a command that made the dogs run even more swiftly as they raced toward the ranch, through the gate, and up to the door.

"Thanks a lot, Fred," Gordon exclaimed. "That was great."

Molly also babbled thanks and then urged Fred to come into the house for coffee.

"Nope. Got to be gettin' back or Sue'll bust a hamepiece. Gordy, you have your ma ready good and early in the morning so's we can get to the McCartys for Christmas Eve doin's."

Molly and Gordon stood watching the dogs through the gate and onto the flat, and then Gordon said, "Well, if we don't have to break road today, we have time for other things. What say we go get Mother a Christmas tree?"

"We won't be here—" Molly began, and then understanding made her eyes go soft. "But, of course. She'd like one anyway—for tonight."

Gordon nodded. "Father always brought her one from the forest. Last year—"

"I know. And this year Christmas is going to be hard for Mother. We must do all we can to—to make it happy."

They skied to the edge of the forest and Gordon dragged home a small but perfect spruce tree, its needles blue-green and shiny, while Molly filled her arms with boughs of fragrant pine. All afternoon they spent decorating the tree, with their mother helping cheerfully, although Gordon sometimes caught a sad look, quickly concealed, in her eyes.

"Isn't it beautiful—our tree?" Molly exclaimed, standing off to look at the finished result, bright with tiny red-paper bells, festooned with strings of popcorn and chains cut from paper, and hung with popcorn balls and Christmas cookies.

"Yes. It is beautiful," Mother said softly. "Thank you, my dears." And that was reward enough for the two conspirators.

As he came into the warm cabin that evening after the chores were done, Gordon decided that the Christmas season anywhere could not possibly be more lovely. Outside a light new snow had begun to fall softly with the dusk. Inside was warmth and pine fragrance and the good odor of spices. Molly had covered the mantel with the greens she had brought from the forest and hung a great wreath in the center of the chimney.

They all spent the early evening working to finish the gifts they were to take to their neighbors. Mother tied the last few threads of bright yarn into the quilt she was making for Sue Curley, while Molly knitted away to put a bright red band into the top of gray wool socks for Lars. There were only a few rows left to knit when they heard the thud of skis against the wall outside.

"Oh, dear, it's Lars," Molly exclaimed, hastily hiding the socks under the cushion on her chair and then hurrying to open the door to his knock.

"I come to spend evening with you," he announced.

"You aren't Lars—you're Santa Claus," Molly bubbled. "With that big pack on your back, all you need is a red nose and a fat face."

Lars laughed as he set his pack on the table and brushed snow from his shoulders. "Beard is white enough for your Santa," he remarked, setting his pack on the table and opening its flaps. "I bring Swedish yule decorations for tying on your tree. For you, Jean, here is an angel—because it is angel you are to feed this old man so many good meals. For the little Molly—animals, because she have love for all the dumb ones. And for you, Gordon—a skier with red flannel cap and red yarn on wrists and ankles for sock and mitten."

One by one he took his gifts from the pack and laid them down on the table. Wooden figures they were, carved and whittled with infinite skill and long patience.

"They are lovely, Lars," Jean Stevens said. "So tiny. So perfect."

From his pack he brought more of the little figures—shaggy dogs, cows and calves, donkeys and camels, horses and colts, and even tiny cocks painted in bright colors. There was a straw Santa Claus driving a team of straw reindeer. There was a straw goat and there were tiny sheaves of wheat intricately carved from wood.

"In Sweden," Lars told Molly, who had been exclaiming with delight over each of the figures, "children put sheaves of wheat out to feed the birds at Christmas time. Here in valley we raise no wheat because of cold, and no birds in winter to eat from sheaves. But I carve one sheaf anyway—for Swedish Christmas."

Last of all he brought out the figure of a tiny elf, his gray beard made from tufts of raveled yarn. The elf rode on the back of a fat and grinning pig.

"He's a darling—pig and all," Molly exclaimed. "What is he, Lars?"

"He is Scandinavian *nissë*, the *tomtë*. Like your Santa Claus, he bring the Christmas gifts to the children of my country."

They hung the tree with the decorations Lars had brought, and then Mother brought corn to pop and cold milk to drink, and they sat before the roaring fire to listen while Lars told stories of Christmas in his country. They sang all the old carols, and Lars taught them a Swedish Christmas song. The evening that Gordon had been dreading for his mother's sake passed happily.

"Stay the night with us, Lars," she insisted.

"Yes, I will stay, Jean. The yuletide is not time an old man like to be alone."

The snow had stopped during the night, and a cloudless sky promised a sunny day. Lars and Gordon milked and then turned the calves into the pens with their mothers.

"So. Calves will milk for you while you are gone," Lars said, chuckling. "They are greedy little feller."

They threw down an extra supply of hay for the stock and shut Pete in the barn with feed and water.

"Have to leave plenty for all the animals," Gordon said. "We'll be gone three or four days. You haven't forgotten that we have to ski to the store to mail out our samples?"

"No, I do not forget," Lars replied, smiling at the eagerness that prompted the question.

They were ready when Fred drove his dogs through the gates at sunrise on the day before Christmas. Gordon helped his mother into the sled, packing around her all the gifts and food she was taking and covering her to the nose with fur robes. Then he and Molly and Lars skied off over the flat, stopping at the meadows to pitch extra hay from the stacks for the cattle herd. At Fred's ranch everybody piled into the body of the hay wagon, mounted on bobsled runners. Sue had heated soapstones for their feet, and Fred had lined the bottom of the wagon with a thick layer of straw and old comforters. With sleigh bells jangling they drove off over the snowy track to the McCartys' ranch, fourteen more miles down the valley.

Big Kate McCarty stood at the door of her warm kitchen to welcome her neighbors. "Merry Christmas, everybody," she called out. "Come in Sue, Jean, Molly. The boys and Matt are down to the barn waiting for you men, and you'll be wanting to put up your horses."

Feeling a little ill at ease, Gordon joined the three Mc-Carty sons—Tim and John and Lou, big-boned, broad-shouldered boys who were always laughing. They were daring riders. On summer Sunday afternoons Gordon had often seen them taming vicious brutes of horses just off the range, sitting their twisting enemies with skill and nerve, laughing as they flapped big cowboy hats to make the horses buck harder. Lou, the youngest one, was a little more quiet than his noisy brothers, and Gordon turned to him, following him about to help with the chores in the huge McCarty barn.

"Hear you're learnin' to ski," Lou said. "Gettin' pretty good?"

"Not good enough to suit Lars."

"Never could learn to manage the things," Lou went on. "I'll stick to webs in the winter and a good horse under me in the summer."

Old Matt McCarty overheard and turned from talking to

Lars and Fred to roar out, "My boys can sure stick to the back of any horse, but put them on them little slats, and they're ridin' with their noses to the snowdrifts the whole time. They were tryin' it the other day, slidin' on a hill behind the house. Down they come, hit a snowdrift at the bottom and dove clean through to come out the other side whiter'n a spilled sack of flour. You're a good lad, Gordy, if you've learned the knack of it."

Gordon felt more at home after Old Matt's praise. It was good to be able to do something that the big McCarty boys could not do. He was over his shyness now, he told himself, and he meant to enjoy every moment of his holiday. And Christmas Eve for him did indeed become a whirl of food and fun. After supper that evening they all gathered to sing carols about the organ, which Kate McCarty played with vigor, and when Old Matt brought out his fiddle, everybody danced. Molly's face was flushed and her pigtails bobbed as she sailed through the turns with one McCarty brother after another, but with Lou the most often, and Gordon was glad to see that even his mother's face had lost its sad look as she danced with big Tim, who really could whirl through a waltz. The old clock wheezed out the stroke of midnight before the merriment was over, and then it was really Christmas Day.

"Having fun?" Gordon whispered to Molly as they waited for the women to settle the argument about where everyone was to sleep.

"Yes, lots," she whispered back. "Only, Gordy, they're all so big and—and vigorous. I guess I'm sort of tired."

Christmas morning everybody was up early for the opening of presents around the great fir tree that stood in one corner of the room. There were gifts for everybody—gifts that had been made from materials to be found in the mountains: braided rawhide reins and bridles fashioned by men for men; and, made by the women, knitted caps and scarfs and mittens, chokecherry jelly, ruby red in the glass, and baskets woven of reed or straw. The gifts most appreciated by Gordon and Molly came from their mother, who had cut down heavy mackinaw trousers that had belonged to their father, tapering the cuffs at the ankles and putting on an elastic to go beneath the foot.

"They're wonderful, Mother," Gordon said. "Snow won't go through this material, and they're just the thing for skiing."

"No more wet socks," Molly chimed in. "We can put them underneath the pants and lace our boots right over everything."

Christmas dinner was a treat of three great stuffed geese, raised from goslings by Kate McCarty and fattened for this day. Sue Curley brought out a huge plum pudding and from one of her capacious apron pockets took a small bottle of brandy to pour around the pudding and light into a blue flame.

"Been hiding this brandy from Fred ever since last summer," she said, winking at her husband over her steel-rimmed spectacles.

After dinner Gordon nudged Lars, and they excused themselves and fastened on the skis they had brought with them in the sled.

"We sink deep in snow," Lars remarked, chuckling as they poled across the flat toward the store-saloon kept by Smiley Tufts. "All that goose and pudding is heavy load for skis."

At the store Lars bought bacon and some tobacco for his pipe. When Gordon gave Smiley the samples, he promised that he would try to get the package out for them as he stowed it on a shelf behind cans of tinned peaches. Gordon heard strange voices coming from the room behind the store, where a long pine slab on log stumps served as a crude bar.

"Who's in there, Smiley?" Gordon asked. Strangers in the valley in wintertime!

"Two outsiders. Been here a week, askin' for old Tom Rider." Gordon looked at Lars in utter panic, but Smiley was going on with his talk. "They was hopin' Old Tom would get kind of dry and mebbe come in for some Christmas cheer. Tom, he ain't come in, though I—"

"Outsiders?" Gordon interrupted impatiently. "How on earth did they get here through all this snow? Nobody except valley people get in and out of here in the winter."

Smiley brushed his cat from the counter with a gentle hand and wrapped up the bacon at which it had been sniffing. The cat yowled in anger, and Smiley said, "Don't you go cussin' me, Tib. Other folks don't love you the way I do."

The cat waved its yellow tail and spoke more harsh words. Smiley grinned toothlessly, reached down a can of milk from the shelf, punched two holes in it, and poured some milk into a saucer on the floor. Tib advanced on the saucer daintily, as Smiley grinned again and wiped milk off on his soiled trousers. He hadn't answered the question.

"Who are they?" Gordon demanded impatiently.

Smiley gazed at his pet foolishly. "Didn't go for to hurt your feelings, Tib cat," he said, watching the pink tongue at work.

"Who did you say those two were?" Gordon prompted, although he knew from experience that Smiley wasn't to be hurried.

"Didn't say. They may be outsiders, but they come in on webs. Good at it too. They ain't no softies. One of 'em's an old prospector, name of Dan Sater. He's took to city ways some, but he ain't forgot how to get around in the

mountains. Purty good man. The other one's Wes Hickson.
I ain't got much time for him. Tib don't take to him."

"But what do they want?" Gordon persisted. "What are
they here for?"

"Don't know as they rightly said, and of course I ain't
asked 'em. I'll tell you one thing though, they're both
mighty interested in Tom Rider."

Gordon was feeling increasing alarm, but Lars said
quietly: "If it is Tom they wait to see, he will not come.
Not this Christmas. Old Tom is dead, Smiley."

"Dead? Say, that's too bad. Well, it happens to all old
prospectors, but Tom was—a mighty good fellow."

"I think it would be well," Lars went on, "if you did
not tell this to these two who ask for him—this Sater and
Hickson. Let them wait for Old Tom to come in—until
they maybe get tired waiting and go away."

Smiley peered quizzically from beneath his beetling
eyebrows for a moment. "Sure," he said. "Sure. If you say
so, Lars."

"And if you just wouldn't mind not saying anything to
them about our package either," Gordon put in eagerly,
"we'd be glad. Don't give it to them to mail if they decide
to go outside. It's—well, it's Tom's business, and it's sort
of private."

"Sure, Gordy. I wouldn't anyway. Never pays to tell outsiders anything about valley affairs. How'd Old Tom die,
Lars? What ailed him? Thought he looked kind of peaked
when he came in here in September to mail a letter out.
To some mining company it was."

Mining company, Gordon thought. Then it was just as
they had guessed, he and Lars. Tom had written this letter
to see if he could sell his claim. And now there wasn't a
doubt but that these two strangers had come to investigate

it. Lars did not seem to be at all bothered; he was telling Smiley about finding Old Tom.

"Goin' off all alone in the hills," Smiley remarked gloomily. "Tain't no kind of life I'd want. Nor death. Want to come on back with me and look those fellers over? I got to feed 'em."

He picked up his cat and set it on his shoulder, and they all walked into the next room, where the two men sat at the bar drinking. The older man, whose blond hair was graying to a muddy yellow, looked up and smiled in a friendly way.

"How are you?" he said. "My name's Sater. And this is my partner, Wes Hickson. You must be Lars Antonsson. I've been hearing about you from Smiley. A Swede, he says, and quite a skier. Who's the kid?"

"This is my good friend, Gordon Stevens. He skis too."

"Good Scotch name. Live here in the valley, boy?"

Gordon answered, "Yes, sir," politely and studied the two men while they talked to Lars. Dan Sater seemed like a frank and honest man, the kind it was hard not to like; but Wes Hickson was lean and swarthy, too quick in his talk and movements, younger but less forceful. He had a— closed face, Gordon told himself, trying to think of the right word, as if some meanness inside should be hidden. Hickson wasn't the man to be particular about the method he used to accomplish whatever he set out to do.

Smiley had shuffled out with his cat to the kitchen in the rear and very soon he came back with two plates loaded with greasy fried potatoes, ham and eggs. Hickson eyed the plate with disgust.

"Ham and eggs," he growled. "For two weeks we've been eating them three times a day. Couldn't you have found us something else for Christmas dinner?"

"Eat 'em and like 'em, or go somewhere else," Smiley

retorted and then grinned as he added, "only there ain't no place else." Leaving Tib on the bar, he shuffled out for coffee.

"Come on back here, old man, and get your blamed cat," Hickson shouted in fury. "I'm not going to eat this dee-licious Christmas dinner with that yellow devil looking on."

"Go hungry then," Smiley shouted back. "Tib's as good as you are. Better, I'm thinkin'."

Tib sat down near Hickson's plate, and the man ate sourly, keeping a wary eye on the cat. Daintily Tib reached out a paw and scooped up a piece of ham. Hickson rose with a roar of anger, picked up Tib by the scruff of the neck, and flung the yowling cat into a corner of the room. Whereupon Smiley came stalking in from the kitchen to dump coffee cups on the table and then scoop up Tib and carry his pet to the kitchen, talking gently to soothe Tib's injured feelings.

"It's time to get out of here," Hickson muttered to his partner. "I'm tired of this waiting around—tired of eating my meals with a cat. I'm sick of these blamed mountains and all this snow. Let's get back to the city."

Dan Sater chewed his dry ham philosophically. "Keep your shirt on, Wes," he advised. "No use getting all riled up over a cat." Then he turned to Lars to ask carefully, "Ever hear of an old prospector around here named Tom Rider?"

There, it was out, Gordon thought. Now the questions would come fast. Better leave the answers to Lars. He was older and wiser, wouldn't lose his head and give things away.

"Yes," Lars replied. "Good friend, Tom Rider."

"So? Where does he live. I—have a message to give him."

"Tom have cabin back in mountains. Long way. Hard

to get there now in all this snow. If you wish, give me the message, and I will be glad to take it up to that cabin."

"No, no. I wouldn't like to bother you. We'll hunt him if he doesn't come in pretty soon."

"Tom will not come. Snow too deep. Gordon, here, is

good on skis. We will both go up to Tom's cabin, take message for you. Skiing is only way to get there now."

"What's the matter with webs?" Hickson broke in. "Webs will go anywhere those fool little sticks of yours will go." He turned to his partner. "We'd better try snowshoeing in, Dan. Find out how to get there from the Swede, will you? You know the country, and I don't."

"Tom's place is hard to find," Lars said mildly. "Trail is covered now with snow. No markers. You will get lost in timber. No, it take ski to get there. Ski go places snow-shoe won't."

"Who says so?" Wes flared angrily. "Dan and I are old hands with the webs, and we can get anywhere in these hills. Bet you ten we could beat you and the kid in a ten-mile race—if you'd set it on flat and uphill some. Maybe you'd pass us going down, but we'd catch up and pass you on the flat. Uphill we'd beat you too. No slipping back. And if the snow happens to be soft, give me webs every time."

Hickson had forgotten all about getting directions to Tom's cabin while he argued the merits of snowshoeing. Gordon grinned at the cleverness of Lars, but he was glad when Banty Clagg came in, stamping the snow from his boots. Banty was a weazened old prospector who lived in a cabin near the store during the winter months. Pushing his battered hat back on his bald head, he slid onto a stool next to Hickson.

"Aren't you afraid that hat'll slide off that marble head-piece of yours and land in the ham and eggs—which is all you'll get?" Wes Hickson asked disagreeably.

Banty was not bothered. "Nope. Been nailed there for a good many years now. A hat's like a good temper, a mighty fine thing to keep fastened on." He turned to the door to shout, "Come on in, Jack. No use hangin' around out there in the cold. These here gentlemen can't hurt you."

Banty's partner shuffled into the saloon. Happy Jack was a huge and gentle man with a dark curling beard and vague eyes. "Teched in the head," the valley people always said of him, "but he never harmed nobody." He came in with a sidewise shambling gait and took the stool on the other side of Banty. When Hickson at once turned his attention to baiting Happy Jack, Lars nudged Gordon and jerked his head toward the door, and they slipped quietly away, strapped on their skis, and were off up the valley.

"You're pretty cute, Lars," Gordon said as soon as he was sure they were out of hearing. "You let Sater think Old Tom was up there, but you never told even a little fib. And then you got Hickson to talking about snowshoeing. And he bragged so hard that he forgot all about getting directions."

"Snowshoer always think he can beat skier," Lars said, his blue eyes twinkling.

"But they've come about the claim, all right. That letter Smiley told us Tom mailed to some mining company. Maybe Sater is the mining company. Do you suppose they'll try to find our claim?"

"Maybe. I think they hunt up Tom—try to."

"And what if Smiley breaks down and tells them Old Tom is dead? Smiley never keeps anything to himself."

"He will not tell. You see what that Hickson do to poor Tib."

"Well, anybody—Banty, or even Happy Jack—could tell them how to find Tom's cabin. Could they do anything to our claim slip—the one we put in the tobacco can?"

"Yes, they could change slip to one for themselves. That is called jumping a claim."

"Would it be theirs then?"

"No. First they would have to take copy to Hailey. File on claim there. We will have to beat them in doing that."

They skied on in silence for a time, and then Gordon said, "I don't like that Wes Hickson. He'd enjoy cheating, even stealing."

"He is man with mean soul," Lars agreed. "But I think

also he is man who talk much about what he will do and then quits when way grows hard. But that older one, that Sater. He is not mean. He must be a little honest or Tom would not have wanted to deal with him. But—he is hard-headed businessman, cheat some to make money."

"Then he would jump our claim."

"I think yes. He will go up there, find Tom gone, figure he is dead. Then maybe find our claim slip and change. He tell himself, 'Smart man makes money.' And like your saying, 'Early bird gets worm,' he try to be first to get to Hailey to file. Big game with him—who gets there first is winner. But if he lose, I think he be what you call good sport."

"Then we just have to keep checking up on our claim, Lars, unless they give up and leave," Gordon said with determination. "And we have to be the winners—somehow."

X

*C*louds formed over the mountains on the day that they returned from the Christmas celebration, and by evening snow fell. For two days it came in swirling fury. Lars remained at home, and Gordon sat by the fire, mending harness, reading, working problems in algebra, and coaching Molly in her arithmetic. On the second day she tired of lessons and brought in pieces of pine to carve into little figures like those Lars had made, but because she was too eager for quick results, she spoiled one after another of her attempts, pettishly dumping her failures into the fire. Gordon was sullen and irritable, for the continued snow made him feel shut in. He was worried too about Sater and Hickson and eager to ski up to the claim again to see if the tobacco can had been molested.

"Quit worrying about your old claim," Molly grumbled crossly. "You know nobody could get up to Tom's in this storm."

"Molly's right, Gordy," his mother said from the couch on which she was resting, for she had not felt well since their return from the McCarty ranch. "The claim is safe enough until this storm is over."

She had been complaining of a pain in her side, saying that no doubt she had overeaten on Christmas Day. Although she insisted that she would be all right in a day or so, Gordon noticed that the little worry lines about her mouth seemed to have deepened and that her face looked pinched and white. Crossing to the western window, he looked out at the place where the mountains should have stood against the sky, but there was nothing to see except gray cloud and the thick veil of the wind-blown snow.

"Storms always come at the wrong time," he complained. "This one is going to keep everybody from leaving the valley, and our ore samples won't get mailed. What's more, all this soft new snow is going to make it hard for Lars and me to get up to Tom's cabin."

"Do stop worrying, Gordy," his mother said. "You're getting cabin fever. Molly, too."

"What's cabin fever?" Molly asked, looking up from her whittling.

Mother smiled. "Oh, that's what these old prospectors get when they're shut up in their cabins, two or them together, for a long winter. I've heard that sometimes they quit speaking to each other, won't cook or eat together. They've even been known to take ax or knife to each other."

"My goodness, Gordy," Molly exclaimed, horrified, "we don't want to be knifing each other." She jumped up impulsively to throw all her whittlings on the fire. "Come on, let's put on our coats and go shovel the snow away from the windows."

They bundled up against the cold wind, and, fastening their skis on at the door, climbed the sloping wall of snow that had slid from the warm roof on two sides of the house. Gordon shoveled away at the snow, digging with vicious strokes, pretending that he was disposing of the storm itself, and he began to feel more cheerful from the fresh air and exercise.

"There's a break in the clouds over the mountains," he told Molly. "See. Maybe it will clear tonight."

"It will, Gordy. I'm just sure it will—for you."

Gordon was pleased—although he wasn't going to let her know it, of course—and a little touched by her wish that everything would come right for him about the claim, even if its success meant unhappiness for her. Ever since he had gone with Lars to hunt the bear, Molly had never again looked at him with disappointment in her eyes. She had faith in him now, and he was going to have to live up to it.

"The sky isn't going to clear just because I want to get up to the claim," he said gruffly in the hope of covering his thought. And she smiled as if she knew exactly what had been in his mind.

Her prediction about the weather proved true. The sun came up the next morning to climb above the last rags of gray cloud and out into blue sky. The thermometer had dropped to twenty below zero, and the sun, although it shone all day, seemed to bring little warmth. That evening a three-quarters moon, sharp and clear, shone down on the reflecting snows to make the night as bright as day.

"I'm going to ski over to see Lars, Mother," Gordon said. "I won't stay. Just long enough to try to talk him into skiing up to Tom's tomorrow—if the good weather holds. Want to come along, Molly?"

She looked wistful, but she shook her head. "I think I'd better stay with Mother because she doesn't feel too well. You go on, Gordy."

The snow glittered in the cold blue moonlight, and the shadows of the near hills lay black and mysterious at the edge of the valley as Gordon glided across the flat. As soon as he rounded the hogback, he could see the point of light from the trapper's window. He took off his skis, stamped the snow from his boots, and the door opened, with Lars framed in the lamplight.

"Come in, boy, come in," he said cheerfully. "It is cold night to be out. But moon is shining bright, and youth like that shadowy brightness. An old man, he like to stay in by fire."

The kitchen table, drawn near the fireplace, held two or three traps, and Gordon saw that his friend had been oiling them, tinkering the sharp jaws. Was Lars preparing for another trapping expedition? Gordon decided that he'd better bring up the subject of his proposed trip at once.

"Look, Lars," he said, "don't you think we ought to ski up to Tom's cabin tomorrow? I know Sater and Hickson couldn't get up there in the storm we've been having, but today maybe they made it. Shouldn't we see if everything is all right?"

Lars did not even take a moment to consider his answer. "No. I have not run trapline for five days. Tomorrow I go to shelter in woods, stay all night, follow circle back next day. Maybe then we go to Tom's."

"But suppose those two are up there right now?"

"They might start in sunshine today, but it will take them two days to get there from Smiley's. They stay somewhere tonight, maybe with Sue and Fred. Tomorrow they be there."

"But shouldn't we be waiting for them when they come? To tell them Tom left the claim to you?"

"That would do no good," Lars answered, chuckling. "If they wish to jump claim, then they just wait until we are not there. Come back later to do their cheating business. No. We let them change claim notice and go away. Then they rest easy once their slip of paper is in tobacco can, sit back and say claim now belong to Dan and Wes. They think we are fools—mountain ignorant. And we smile—and go change claim back to our name."

"They'll take samples back with them to send the assayer."

"Certainly they will. But then they must wait, same as we do. They sit and eat Smiley's ham and eggs—with cat. Stay in out of cold. Pat each other on back because claim is theirs."

"But suppose they go on out of the valley and file on the claim?"

"That they will not do. Trip not worth risk unless they know about ore. They will wait for assayer's report to see if ore is rich. If ore not rich, then maybe they try to buy up some other claim. One from Banty Clegg, maybe. Always he is trying to sell. No, Gordon, we will stay here and do our work."

Knowing that he had to be satisfied to wait, Gordon offered to help Lars run his trapline, but Lars said, "No, you have ranch work to do. I know that. And your mother—she is not well."

Lars was right about the work, and the next day Gordon took the hayrack off its wheels and mounted it on bobsled runners to break out a trail to the cattle shelter in the meadow. Filling the rack with hay from the stacks, he scattered it over the snow for the cattle, circling widely to spread the feed well over the field near the shelter. He hauled two loads of hay from the stack to the barn for the horses and the two cows that provided milk for the family. With Molly he practiced skiing on the flat and hills near the road so that they could keep watch for the mining men, but they saw no sign of the snowshoers. The waiting, Gordon told himself, at least had given his mother time to recover until she was feeling almost as fit as ever.

They started for Tom's cabin the morning after Lars returned from his trip. As they turned into the opening of the trail, they saw tracks leading from the forest edge toward the path.

"They've been here all right," Gordon said. "Snowshoe marks."

"They have been up, yes. And come down not too long ago. See, tracks pointing up have little snow drifted in. Tracks coming down are fresh."

"Sneaks! They went around through the timber, trying to hide. I suppose that's why Molly and I didn't see them go by."

Lars had been studying the tracks. "They are good snowshoers, those two."

"How can you tell? You've never seen them doing it."

"Tracks are regular. Not erratic. Good steady snowshoers have make these track."

"Let's hurry, Lars," Gordon urged. "I want to see what they've done."

"Why hurry? They are gone and will not come back. We know what they do up there—change paper we leave in can. And that is what we want."

Lars kept Gordon to a slow and steady pace of climbing until at dusk they reached the cabin.

"Well, one thing those crooks did for us anyway," Gordon remarked. "They left us a packed trail with their snowshoes. We'd never have made it by this time if we'd had to break snow all day."

Lars was examining the tracks around the cabin. The clearing was crisscrossed with the marks of webs as if their wearers had gone here and there in their search.

"They have troubles, I think," Lars said, nodding his head with satisfaction. "Our claim, it is not easy to find. Tomorrow we go see. Now it is too dark."

"Golly, Lars," Gordon exclaimed, "there's something I just this minute thought of, or I'd have worried more than I did. Do you suppose Old Tom sent directions to them? Or why would they even look for the claim? They'd know they couldn't find it if they didn't know where to start—not with a whole mountain to cover—and all this snow."

"I think he gave them a hint because he knew he was ill. Then he begin to think maybe he not trust them, and he fix up hidden blaze, and write that note for me. Tomorrow we find out."

The cabin had been lived in. Dirty dishes crowded the table, bacon congealing on the plates. Lars sniffed at the coffeepot, half full of stale coffee and cooked grounds. Disgust on his face, he emptied the contents out the door and came back to begin scouring the pot.

"They didn't leave any kindling cut, the way we did," Gordon complained. "And they've tracked snow and mud in and not swept out. The bed isn't made and—"

"They are untidy men, those two. Careless of comfort for any but themselves."

Gordon was looking at the tracks on the floor with suspicion. "Hey, Lars, how did they get mud on their boots? In all this snow? They've found our claim—been digging in it."

Lars said comfortably, "It is likely. But we fix. To-morrow."

The next morning they found that the snowshoe tracks circled the cabin a couple of times and led off in wrong directions, as if the mining men had been at first confused. Evidently they had soon recovered, for the prints went in a direct line toward the blazed tree and on toward the claim.

"How did they find the way so quickly?" Gordon asked in astonishment.

"They have follow our old ski tracks. I tell myself they would do that. See, our tracks are covered up with snow, but there is a little sinking where we ski. They follow that depression in snow, and it lead them right to claim." He laughed at Gordon's crestfallen expression. "But that is what we want them to do. Now we can go take their paper out of tobacco can. Put ours in."

As they neared the tunnel, Gordon could see a pile of fresh earth blackening the snow all around the opening. "They've dug around in there all right."

"Yes. For samples to send to assayer."

Gordon skied swiftly to the pile of rocks that held up stake and tobacco can and, opening the can, took out a fresh slip of paper, a claim to the diggings in the name of Dan Sater and Wes Hickson. The writing was bold, and the wording was better than that Gordon had used. Gordon read the paper aloud.

"The old cheats!" he exclaimed.

Lars was cheerfully unconcerned. "Write the slip over, boy, and put in our names. We will just—smart-out those two. And we must make a copy to show the location of the claim when we file."

On the way down the home trail, Lars and Gordon agreed that now they must hurry to file on their claim. They dared not wait for the summer sun to clear the pass.

"When the report on our samples come back—soon, I hope," Lars said, "then we will ski over the pass. I know that now you can ski that steep slope on other side."

As they neared the ranch, Gordon saw with alarm that there was a light shining from every window, even one in the bedroom, which was always kept closed off in the winter and heated only when some member of the family was ill.

"It's Mother. She's sick again, Lars," Gordon muttered, putting all his strength into his poles to increase his glide.

A white-faced, frightened Molly flung open the door as soon as she heard the thud of their skis on the wall. "Oh, Gordy, I'm so glad you've come," she said, almost crying. "Mother's awfully sick. Go talk to her, Gordy. And Lars, see if you can help her. She hurts so, and I couldn't do anything to stop it."

Gordon hurried into the bedroom, followed by Lars. Jean Stevens lay in bed, her face drawn with pain, her hands pressed to her abdomen.

"I'm glad you're here, Gordy," she gasped. "I—I worried."

Gordon looked down at her, feeling a sick helplessness. Illness here in the mountains, even a small illness, was frightening. Cruel miles of unbroken snow lay between the ranch and a doctor's help, and no doctor, even if one could be reached, would be willing or able to attempt the four-thousand-foot barrier of the mountain. In growing panic he watched while Lars probed the distended abdomen with strong, gentle fingers. Mother winced.

"It hurts there, Jean?" Lars asked. "This spot is sore?"
She nodded.

"The pain, it is bad? Sharp?"

"Sometimes. And all the time a—dull hurt."

Lars straightened from his examination. "Do you have hot water bottle, Molly?"

"Yes, I'll go put the kettle on."

"No. Gordon, you go out, fill bottle with snow. Not too much. Bag must not be heavy. Bring back quickly."

Lars placed the filled bag over the tender place. "That will help, Jean. Could you drink a quart of buttermilk?"

"I could try. Things don't—stay down."

Molly brought fresh buttermilk from the last churning, and while his patient sipped, Lars walked to the kitchen, followed by Gordon.

"Is it bad, Lars?" he asked, afraid to hear the answer.

"Bad enough. But it does not mean danger, I think. She have infection in appendix. Light attack. I will stay, and we will try the snow pack and buttermilk. If it get worse—"

"What then? If it gets worse?"

"I do not know. Toboggan over mountain, maybe. You and I on ski to pull her. But that would be—danger. Too slow, too. Better we wait." He hesitated and then went on slowly, as if in doubt. "I do not know much about knife, which is job for experienced surgeon. But if it is necessary, I would try. I have watch it done."

Gordon turned away, sick with fear. Although he had great faith in Lars, the thought of a knife in an unpracticed hand was not bearable. He took the milk pails and walked to the barn, for the cows must be milked, and Molly would be more help in the house than he would. Another cold night, he thought. A full moon cleared the eastern mountains to shine on the great peaks. The remote summits gleamed stark and ghostly, making him feel entrapped and helpless. Those white walls shut the valley from aid as effectively as if they had been made of steel.

He finished the milking and carried in the pails, mechanically pouring the milk into the flat pans in the lean-to. Although he tried to eat the meal that Molly had prepared, the food tasted like straw in his mouth, and he pushed back his plate and went to the fire.

Through the night he and Lars watched beside the bed. Gordon kept the fires roaring and refilled the bottle with snow as the fever of his mother's body melted the contents. She slept fitfully, waking occasionally to cry out in pain, but toward morning the pain came less often. At dawn she fell into a deeper slumber.

Lars put a gentle hand on her forehead. "The fever have gone away. Forehead is moist now. She will get better soon. Go to bed, boy, and sleep. I will doze here in this chair beside her. Danger, I think, is over—for this time."

Gordon climbed the ladder to his loft and crawled wearily under the covers without undressing. He awoke at dawn to stumble down to the kitchen, rubbing from his eyes the sleep he had not finished.

"I did the milking," Molly said, looking happy and relieved. "Mother's awake and lots better."

"Lars?"

"In there with her. Go talk to her, Gordy."

He went in to stand wordlessly beside his mother. She smiled at him, and he saw that a little color had come back into her face, as she sat propped up in bed with a white wool shawl wrapped around her shoulders.

"Don't look so woebegone, Gordy," she said. "I'm all right now that the pain is gone. Lars is a good doctor. A good friend too—more than a neighbor. What was the matter with me, Lars?"

"It is your appendix, Jean, but a light attack."

Gordon saw his mother's brows draw together in fear, and her color went swiftly away.

"Oh, no, Lars. No. Will there be—other times?"

"Perhaps. We must be careful all the rest of winter because—here in mountains—we cannot get you to a doctor without danger. Maybe you have other light attack or so, and those I can pull you through. But when summer come, when mountain road is open, then I think we must take you to town and have out this offender. Living the way we do, penned here in mountain snow, it is not safe to let that appendix stay to make more trouble."

"An operation, Lars? Oh, no—we can't—"

Gordon knew that it was not fear of the surgeon's knife that had turned his mother's face so white; for herself she was always brave enough. She was thinking that they would have no money in the summer to pay a doctor's fee. Eight dollars and sixty-three cents was all they had, and there would be no more until they could sell the steers after the fall drive. Even if they waited and used the cattle money for the operation, there would be no funds with which to buy food for the next winter. They had only one chance.

"The Molly Mine, Mother," he spoke out abruptly. "Our claim. We've got to sell it. If the ore is rich—if we can only beat Sater and Hickson to filing, then maybe— Lars, do you suppose those two would buy our claim?"

"They might. I think they have interest themselves much in this claim. Tom's letter maybe promise big wealth. If they had not wanted to buy from him, then they would not have come to this valley in winter. They will try to get by crooked means first, and if no success, maybe buy from us."

"Do you suppose they have money?" Gordon asked hopefully.

"I think so. They have good clothes. Expensive boots, handmade. I see that. And they stay at Smiley's long time. Have plenty for food and drinking."

"Then we must hurry to file on our claim. We can't wait, Lars. Let's ski out over the south mountain—just as soon as Mother is well for sure. Let's not wait for their samples to come back, or ours either. It might be months before we hear, if nobody gets out with our package for a long time."

"No. Ore may be no good. Then our trip out would be effort wasted. We wait for letter from assayer."

"Of course you must wait, Gordy," his mother put in hastily. "To take that dangerous trip for nothing—that would be sheer folly. I—I don't want you to go at all. I wish—"

He saw that his mother was upset, and he knew that she was thinking of the vast slopes that lay on the other side of the mountain barrier. About those slopes he did not like to think, for he wasn't sure that he could run them safely.

"Lars, why couldn't we just ski out through the canyon, go around the mountains," Gordon suggested hopefully, although he knew the safer, easier way was in reality impractical.

The trapper gave him one brief, scornful look before he shook his head. "Take too long. Two weeks, maybe three, and that much back again. We do not dare leave Jean alone with Molly for that time. Besides, too much flat for skiing. We go over mountain in one day."

Gordon gave up his idea reluctantly, rose, and motioned for Lars to follow him out of the bedroom. While they ate a belated breakfast, Lars kept shaking his head over the vast amounts of bacon and eggs, pancakes and milk that Gordon was consuming. Molly, feeling important because she was in charge of the kitchen, stood over the hot stove turning cakes and rushing them to the table, her pigtails pinned up out of the way, her face rosy with her haste and zeal.

"My cakes are all right, Lars, Gordy?" she asked eagerly. "They're good, aren't they?"

Gordon pretended to frown. "A little heavy, but we're eating them." But when he saw her crestfallen expression, he added quickly, "Aw, Molly, I was only teasing. They're mighty good, and—well, you're doing fine with Mother's work."

She smiled, flushing with pleasure, but she said seriously, "If you can take Father's place, I can take Mother's."

Gordon did not respond to that remark, but he let her see his pride in her with a quick look. There wasn't any need for words anyway, he told himself, since she always seemed to read his mind. But just to show his approval of her cooking, he took another stack of cakes.

Lars said slyly, "If Molly's cakes are heavy, then your skis will ride deep this morning. You have big oat bin for stomach."

"He didn't eat a bit of dinner," Molly defended. "Of course he's hungry now that Mother's better."

Satisfied at last, Gordon pushed back his chair and returned to the subject of the claim. "Look, Lars, we can't just sit here and do nothing about filing. The money means too much now for Mother."

"I have something to tell you," Lars began, looking mysterious. "This I have not say to you before because I did not want you to hope and then be disappoint. I think I tell you now."

"What, Lars? Tell me what." Lars could certainly be exasperating at times.

"The report on our samples will be back sooner than you believe. Tim McCarty, he have girl in Custer, that big mining town downcanyon and up the Yankee Fork. He tell me after we get back from Smiley's that he plan to snowshoe out next day to see her. Same day we came home after Christmas. Storm was coming then, but Tim is not afraid of snow. He would go, he say, storm or no storm. And mail goes out from Custer. They keep road open to there all winter."

"Good! Did you tell him to pick up our package at Smiley's?"

"I tell him. By this time samples are in hands of assayer, and maybe report is on way back. Big Tim promise me to wait for answer. He was glad of excuse to see his girl more. He will be back tomorrow, maybe. Or next day."

Gordon's thoughts churned. He was happy, relieved, and excited, all at the same time, aware also of a new feeling of confidence. The ore would assay high, they would sell the claim for big money. Money for the operation. Money enough so that he could take his mother east to towns and safety where, if illness struck, there would be a doctor to keep danger away. He was so happy in his planning that he forgot to worry about the slopes on the other side of the mountain.

Elated, he told Lars, "Then when Tim gets back with our letter, we can ski over the pass right away. We can file on our claim before Sater and Hickson even get a report on their samples. Let's ski over to meet Tim tomorrow."

"You are forgetting, boy. Your mother is still ill, and we must wait until recovery is sure. Illness must not come again while we are gone."

"Well, heck, I'll go alone then, and you stay here with Mother."

"No. Jean will want you here. She is too ill to be upset by worry about you. When she is safe, then I will be the one to ski alone to meet Tim."

XI

Two days later Lars decided it was safe for him to leave his patient to ski to the McCarty ranch although he made Mother promise to rest in bed and to continue drinking buttermilk.

"Buttermilk is old remedy, Jean," he told her. "Drink all you can. Gordon, if pain come again to your mother, use the rubber bottle filled with snow. In two days I will be back."

It was three days before Lars skied in at dusk, waving a letter jubilantly over his head as he came gliding through the ranch gate. Gordon was so excited and impatient to know the news that he did not wait to put on his own skis, but floundered through the deep snow on foot to meet the trapper.

"The ore?" he shouted. "Is it rich, Lars? Is it?"

"It is ruby silver—like I say. High-grade ore. Assay four hundred to six hundred ounce to ton."

"Golly! Then if we can sell, there'll be money. That's good rich ore, isn't it, Lars?"

"Rich enough for all your needs. For myself I do not care for this money, but for you and Jean to have is good right now."

Sudden doubt gripped Gordon's mind as he thought of

all the chances that stood between him and this money that was to make his mother well again.

"What if Sater and Hickson won't buy?" he asked. "And they can still beat us to the filing."

"Maybe they don't buy, but somebody will. Assayer say claim ought to sell. Good claim, he say. Bring maybe $40,000. Here, you can see for yourself."

After Gordon had read the letter, he wanted to start over the mountain the very next day, but Lars said, "No. If this thaw keep up, to ski the mountain will be easier in few days. Snow have melt a little on top today with warm sun we have. Freeze hard tonight and make crust for easy going. Thaw is good thing for us. And while we wait, I can run my trapline again."

Since his mother seemed to be completely recovered, Gordon went with Lars. The early morning skiing across the flat was fun, for the crust held them up, one stroke carrying them far. The frost crystals that had formed on top crunched under their flying skis to send up a little cloud of white smoke behind them. Across the valley the mountains loomed a glittering white, the blue shadows in the gulches stood out sharp and clear, and the pines below timberline were frosted into silver from the moisture in the wisps of white clouds that floated lazily just below the summits. As the two skiers glided across the flat, the mists drifted up and vanished like rags of smoke into the air. In the morning sunlight the mountains seemed to smile kindly down upon the valley.

They stayed the night in the cabin, keeping the fire roaring up the chimney as protection against the icy air of the high altitude.

"Warm sunny day, Arctic night—that is just what we want now," Lars said.

In the morning they worked along the ridges to follow

the trapline, coming down in the late afternoon to the canyon with its softer snows under the trees, where the sun had not struck to form a crust. Lars was ahead when they came to the last long slide over an open hillside, gleaming red in the light of the setting sun. Gordon, following, felt his skis pitch forward in sudden swift flight as they hit the crust of the open snows. He almost lost balance and fell but recovered quickly. Ahead, he could see Lars flying down toward the flat, enjoying the speed of his run after the slower skiing under the trees. But suddenly the trapper pitched violently and fell with one ski caught in the snow behind him.

"A breakthrough in the crust," Gordon muttered to himself, and watched for Lars to rise.

But there was no quick recovery. For a few seconds he lay still and then tried to struggle out of his tangle, but he did not get up. Alarmed, Gordon sped toward his friend, dropping one knee low to swing into a telemark stop.

"You hurt, Lars?" he asked in frightened solicitude. "What's wrong?"

"It is my ankle, I think. But I have twist knee pretty bad also. Take off my ski."

Hastily Gordon dug in the snow until he could unfasten the binding on the buried ski. When he had released the foot, he helped Lars to a sitting position and unlaced the boot so that Lars could explore the injured ankle.

"It is not the ankle. Not broken," Lars remarked with an effort at cheerfulness. "We put some snow on him and tomorrow will be all right. Help me get up. Take off other ski too."

But when he tried to rise, he only fell back deeper in his flounder. "It is the knee," he explained. "It will not hold my weight. Tendons pulled, maybe."

Gordon looked out over the darkening flat and felt overwhelmed with the hopelessness of their situation. Miles still lay between them and the ranch, and by the time he could ski there to bring back the toboggan, the night cold would have come creeping down from the mountains. The ankle would swell so that the boot would not go back on, and the foot would freeze. Now the sun had set, the cold would soon be vicious enough to freeze a man into death. Lars— Panic that weakened his spirit and strength rose in Gordon like a dark tide.

"What can we do, Lars?" he asked. "We're five miles from the ranch. And this cold—"

"Keep your head, boy," Lars said quietly. "Reach in my pack. See if there is a strap. Long one. I should have put him in."

Gordon searched the pack, fingers fumbling in his haste. "No strap. No thongs of any kind. Just an old piece of baling wire. What did you want the strap for?"

"To fasten skis together. Make toboggan. This old man have grown careless to leave out strap which is always useful to skier."

Hope stimulating his mind to ingenuity, Gordon ripped off his leather belt. "How about this?" he asked. "Yours, too?"

"Good. Now you begin to use head. We will make them do. These and the wire."

Under instructions from Lars, Gordon fastened the trapper's skis together by running the wire through the bindings, lacing them together with it over the top.

"That way wire will not keep skis from running smooth over snow," Lars explained.

"Let's get you up out of that flounder now," Gordon suggested, setting the improvised toboggan close.

Half lifting, half pulling, with Lars helping as much as he could, Gordon managed to get him onto the skis. Then he linked the two belts together by the buckle of one, the holes in the other.

"Not long enough for a pull rope," he muttered in disappointment. "The toboggan ski tips would ride over the ends of mine."

"Lengthen with a pole," Lars suggested.

"Sure. Why didn't I think of that? We can use both of your poles."

Gordon found another small piece of wire in the pack and wired the rings of the two poles together, making a loop of the two belts through the handle of one pole.

"There," he said. "Now you can hang onto the belt loop, and I'll pull you along by the handle of the first pole. Let's try our toboggan."

Darkness had come down before they started the long trek to the ranch, and the bite of mountain cold already nipped at hands and feet and faces. On the narrow sled

Lars rode with his legs thrust out in front of him, one hand behind him on the skis holding him on, the other clinging to the looped belts. The skis slipped over the snow, sinking a little with the old man's weight, but following well enough for progress. When the temperature began to drop rapidly, Gordon stopped to peel off his jacket and fasten it about Lars.

"Work will keep me warm," Gordon said, laughing off objections. "Here, take my muffler too. Wrap it around your foot. With no boot on, that foot will soon freeze."

"That is better, boy. My foot, it is pretty cold. The night is bitter, when I sit and not move."

Gordon struggled on toward the ranch, finding the skiing difficult with only one pole and one arm to help him forward over the flat.

"Stop a minute, boy," Lars called. "I have idea." He peeled off his own long muffler. "Here, take this. Wind

one end around waist and put other end through hand loop on pole you are pulling with. Then you have two arm, two pole to work with."

"But, where is my other pole? I must have left it back there where you fell."

Lars chuckled. "No, I have him. I drag him behind me all the time. See, by the handle loop over my wrist."

They went faster after that. Finally Gordon pulled up at the ranch door and called to Molly for help. When she opened the door, he saw the concern on her face, but she did not exclaim, only helped lift Lars to his feet so that he could hop on his one good leg, with their support, into the kitchen and to the couch by the fire. Gordon threw on more wood and asked his mother to bring cold water in which to soak the swollen ankle. After Lars had warmed, he probed at his injuries.

"Ankle is only little sprain," he said, "but big trouble is in knee. Tendons are pulled all right."

In the struggle to get his friend safely to the ranch, Gordon had forgotten the claim and the trip they had planned over the mountain, but now he started to worry. If Lars could not ski, they could not go. Would they dare wait for the knee to heal? If they did, Sater and Hickson would get ahead of them, file on the claim, and then there would be no money to divide, no operation for his mother; she would have to stay on at the ranch until some more severe attack took her life away. In an effort to shut his mind against that thought, he asked, "How soon do you suppose you'll be able to ski, Lars?"

"I do not know. One month, maybe. Or two. Old men do not heal quickly, like youth."

"Then—we can't ski out over the mountain. And those mining men will get our claim."

"I am afraid that is true. I am sorry, boy."

Gordon stood silent, thinking fast and hard, one question uppermost in his mind. Did he dare to attempt the trip by himself? But skiing alone in the mountains, Lars had told him, was dangerous. Tonight's accident had proved that. If Lars had been alone, he'd be out there now freezing to death. Through Gordon's mind then flashed pictures of the tremendous slopes on the other side of the mountain, the snows that dropped down and down to the valley beyond the barrier. How could he run those steep pitches alone? No, he could slog along over the flat, he could climb the mountain, but the down way he dared not attempt.

He looked at his mother, silent in the big chair by the fire. She looked frail, and there were dark shadows still lingering beneath her eyes. If they lost the claim— If his mother died because her son had not enough courage to face the mountain— Gordon's whirling thoughts came to a sudden stop there.

"I'm going alone," he said.

His mother cried out sharply. "No, Gordy. No. You'll not go without Lars."

"I—I guess I'd make it all right, Mother. I can ski pretty well now."

"No. I can't let you. You might fall, as Lars did tonight. And if you were alone—a broken leg—this terrible cold— And what if the snow should slide? Your father—"

"But the money for your operation—" Gordon began, feeling his determination weaken.

"Money isn't worth a life as precious as yours is to me. The operation can wait until we sell the steers in the fall."

"But, Mother," Gordon protested, "you know that won't do. Where would we get cash to buy next winter's food?"

"We'll sell all the cattle, if need be. But you're not going."

"Sell all the cattle?" Molly said. "We can't have a ranch

without cattle. Next year there wouldn't be any money at all."

"Then we'll just hitch up Bonny and Camp to the wagon and drive all the way to the East," Mother said extravagantly, her lips making a thin straight line of firmness. "But you'll not ski that mountain alone."

"Your mother is right, Gordon," Lars said. Pulling his pipe from his pocket, he filled it, and tamped down the tobacco carefully. "It is good that you have the courage to say you will go. But I tell you once—remember?—that to run toward danger is folly. To ski alone on trail like that one over mountain is also folly. If accident come—no help."

Molly jumped up from her stool beside the fire. "I'll go with you, Gordy," she offered. "I can ski too, you know."

He looked his sister over, considering for a long moment this new possibility. Could she manage the slopes, the long skiing on soft or crusted snow? Could she endure? He almost thought that she could. Feet planted sturdily on the hearth, her body strong and sinewy from ranch life, eyes and chin determined, she looked as if she might be able to do anything that she set out to do. But she was a girl, and the trail over the mountain was long and difficult.

He shook his head regretfully. "No, Molly. You—you're just not good enough on skis. You'd slow me. And anyway, you couldn't make it—not that long a trip. No girl could."

"I can too make it." Molly whirled on Lars. "You know I can, Lars. And I am too good enough on my skis. Tell Gordy so, Lars."

"Yes, Molly," Lars said quietly. "You are skilled enough."

"And I'm every bit as strong as you are, Gordy. Almost, anyway. I've been practicing every day, all the time you two were fooling around with your old claim and the trapping. I can do ten or fifteen miles now, and not even feel tired. And if I slow you on the flat and the up, Gordy, then I'll pass you on the downslopes. I'm going. I can—"

"No. You are not to go, Molly," Mother interrupted, sounding harsh in her determination. "Neither you nor Gordy. Think, Gordy, think. If something should happen to you—or Molly! Do you remember that mail carrier—Slim Brownson? Remember how he fell carrying mail from one mining camp to another? And when they found him the next spring, the coyotes had picked his bones clean. And your father, Gordy. There might be other snowslides to catch you and Molly. You'd never get there, Gordy. Never. You simply can't go. That's settled."

Standing up, she wrapped her shawl about her and walked to her bedroom, moving rapidly as if in her own mind the matter had been determined by her fears and her refusal. Gordon sat in silence, feeling all resolution, all courage ooze from him.

He began telling himself that he hadn't been too eager to take this dangerous trip anyway. Perhaps it would be better just let the claim go to others. He could try to make the money for the operation in some other way—trapping, maybe. After all, he wasn't eager to risk his life on those great downslopes—and certainly not Molly's.

Lars, too, sat in silence, puffing on his pipe and watching Gordon. Molly went to stoke the kitchen stove with more wood, slamming shut the heavy iron door with unnecessary clatter. She came back then to stand in front of her brother, her chin stubborn, her blue eyes steady.

"We could do it together, Gordy. I know we could. If you got ahead of me, we'd just keep each other in sight. That way, we'd be safe enough. Wouldn't we, Lars?"

"Yes, you would be safe enough. And you would make it—with care. I know that."

Gordon thought again of all the dangers his mother had

pointed out, and he said weakly: "Well, look, Lars. Maybe we ought not to try it. Mother is right. All kinds of things can happen—skiing. Molly might get hurt, and—"

Lars took his pipe from his mouth. "Is your fear for Molly, boy? Or is it for yourself? You do not wish to go now. Is that true?"

"Well, yes. If I'm going to be honest, I suppose I'll have to say that I'm afraid to go."

"But you did not feel the scare before Jean have paint for you such a picture of mail carriers and coyotes and bones?"

"A little. The other side is so steep. But I would have tried it—if Mother hadn't put her foot down. What she said made me see how really dangerous the trip would be, made me more afraid."

"I could see that. You are almost fifteen now. Soon you will be a man. How long will you let a woman rule you with her foolish fears?"

Gordon looked up, startled. "What's Mother got to do with it? I suppose you think I'm a—a coward. But if a fellow's afraid inside himself, it isn't his mother's fault."

"I am not sure that it is not Jean's fault. I have never think you were coward. You remember, I have told you that more than once. But always you let your mother talk you into being afraid. She fears to lose you because she still hold on to dread of mountains and snow from losing her Jim. Those fears she plant in your mind. She tell you to be scared—and you listen. Keep on listening, and someday you will be—real coward."

Gordon was angry. He almost hated this old man who was strong enough to tell the truth. The truth? Was it true that his mother was making him into a coward? One by one the times when he had started to act without fear came back to him. And even if he wasn't kept from doing what he felt he ought to do, didn't he always act with fear inside of him? It was true: by her words, even by the expression on her face sometimes, she could suggest panic to him. He glanced at the old man by the fire and felt resentment die.

"I guess you're right, Lars," Gordon said. "But what can I do? She's my mother. And I love her."

"Of course, she's our mother, and we both love her," Molly broke in. "But we don't have to listen when she tells us we have to be afraid. I don't. Oh, yes, I do listen, because it wouldn't be polite and respectful not to. But then—well, I just go ahead and do what I know I have to. And after it's all over, Mother always says I've done the right thing. She's a scaredy-cat for us, Gordy."

"Jean should not pass her fears on to you, Gordon," Lars said thoughtfully. "If you let her keep on doing this, it will destroy you."

"Do you think that—if I'd go on this trip—even if she is afraid to have me go—maybe she might see what she is doing to me?"

"I hope that she will. But if she do not, then we must tell her."

"All right. I'll go." Gordon made up his mind quickly before he could remember again those steep mountain slopes. "And Molly, you'll go with me. We'll do the best we can—together."

Molly's face lit up with her satisfaction, but in a moment it clouded. "But who will do the chores, with Mother ill? And you so you can't get around, Lars?"

"I will stay until you come back. I leave plenty hay for my old horse. He will not starve. And Jean is strong enough to pull me to barn on toboggan for a few days. Soon I can walk again, but not on ski."

Molly found bandages for Lars and bound his knee

tightly, according to his directions. Gordon brought in the skis to wax them and to check the bindings. Lars, at his chair by the fire, took off the ankle straps on his own skis and put them with a small kit of tools into Gordon's pack.

"So," he said. "If binding break, you will be able to mend. Straps, wire, to fix toboggan from skis, we put them in this time. Gordon, do you remember Finnish Matt? That trapper who live at foot of mountain on other side?"

"Yes. What about him?"

"If you need help, he will give. He is good man. Now you must listen. I will tell you this when Jean is not around to take scare. This is dangerous trip—long way, steeper drops than either of you have ski before. You must not get separated. Slow your pace, Gordon, to match Molly's. And no matter what happen, keep your head. Do not ski too fast. Always you must be master of your skis. Now you must both go to bed and sleep for few hour. I will sit here by fire to watch the time. I will call you when it is one o'clock. You must get early start to use hard crust on snow."

XII

At one o'clock in the morning Lars called Gordon and Molly, and they slipped quietly into the kitchen to finish preparations for the mountain trip. Gordon built the fire and hung wool socks over the door of the warming oven, setting the two pairs of boots on top, for it would never do to start with cold feet. Molly made hot chocolate and took out bread for toast, and eggs and bacon.

When Lars began talking in his usual tone, Gordon whispered in alarm, "Hush, please. You'll wake Mother up. If we can slip off without her knowing, she won't have another chance to object to our going."

"That would be wrong, boy," Lars said. "Perhaps her fears have made you afraid sometimes, but not to tell her— that would be another kind of cowardice in you. You must call your mother and give her a chance to say good-by to you."

Without a word of protest Gordon turned to the bedroom. When she came out, belting her robe about her and looking frightened, he hated having to tell her that he and Molly must cross the mountain on their skis. But he did, and the result was what he had expected.

"No, Gordy. I can't let you do this," his mother said, the

thin, pinched look that he dreaded driving the sleepy soft-
ness from her face.

"But we have to go, Mother. The money—"

"No money in the world means as much to me as your
safety and Molly's. If one of you should fall—break a leg
perhaps—then the other one could never bring help before— Gordy, think. The—the coyotes would come, if you
were helpless. Even wolves."

Before he had time to stop the weakening thoughts, Gordon's mind began to make horrible pictures of Molly and
him, freezing in the arctic night. He saw slinking wolves
creep from the pines, felt their red gaze, heard their circling feet. And then he remembered. He was not going to
let his mother suggest fear to him ever again. Besides,
there really wasn't any danger from wolves.

"I'm sorry, Mother, but I'm going," he said firmly.
"Molly, too. I have to go. Can't you see that if—if I don't
go—then I'm always going to know that I was afraid of a little danger? You wouldn't want me to have to know that
about myself. Would you, Mother?"

"You'd be alive, knowing it. What good will it do you to
die knowing you have courage? And anyway, the brave
person doesn't go around hunting danger—taking foolish
chances—"

Gordon turned helplessly to Lars for support. The old
trapper was working on the bindings of Gordon's skis,
white head bent to the yellow light from the lamp. He did
not say much, but his words were a whiplash of scorn.

"When come time to take chance—then take. But only
when much depend, and that time is now. Jean Stevens,
with your own fears you saddle your son. For a year you
have try to make coward of this boy. Is it so that your brave
man, Jim Stevens, would have wish?"

Gordon saw his mother's eyes close for a moment under

the shock of the quiet words, but when she opened her eyes again, they were steady. The tension eased from her shoulders as she straightened them, and she marched toward the stove, her head held high.

"Go get yourself ready to go, Molly," she said sharply. "I'll finish making breakfast."

A half hour later Gordon and Molly slipped into their skis before the cabin door in the icy cold of two o'clock winter morning. As they laced the canvas housings tightly over boots and woolen trousers, the frost bit into bare hands.

"Must be thirty below zero," Gordon muttered to Lars, who had hobbled to the door.

"It is cold, yes," Lars responded calmly. "That is good. The crust will hold until you have cross the mountain."

Gordon patted the pocket into which he had pinned the copy of the claim slip, and then shrugged into the small pack filled under the trapper's directions with cold meat, bread, soup frozen into a small pan, a woods hatchet, waxing dope, screws and screw driver, the extra bindings, matches, a candle stub, extra socks. They would be ready for anything, Gordon thought, anything from a broken binding to a forced camp for the night. Pulling the sheepskin flaps of his cap down over his ears, he drew on his mittens, heavy leather ones with wool linings and then turned to his sister.

"Ready, Molly? Bundle up good. Put your muffler up around your face as much as you can."

"Ready," she answered. And he knew that she was, and would be, ready for anything the night or the day might bring.

Pete whined and jumped, begging to go along, and Mother came, shawled, from the lighted warmth of the cabin to hold the dog's collar.

"Be careful, Gordy," she began. "You must not take

foolish—" She stopped short then and added, "Take care of your sister. Good luck, son."

"You will make it, easy," Lars called as Gordon dug his poles into the snow and cruised off over the iced crust of the sloping meadow in a long sweeping curve. He looked over his shoulder to see that Molly had shoved off and was riding his tracks over the colorless snow of the night. There was no moon, but in the clean black sky the uncountable frosty stars flung a vast sparkling vault above jagged peaks that seemed to thrust heavenward to meet the stars. Moments later they reached the flat, and Molly pushed up to trudge beside her brother.

"How's your gear feel?" he asked.

"All right. How's yours?"

He nodded, for talking hurt in the cruel cold. They glided on in silence. He glanced ahead to the gigantic, stolid might of the barrier mountain that they must cross. Secure in strength and power, it seemed to be waiting for the two pitiful black pinpricks that were Molly and he, waiting for them to ride across the blue-white plain and climb into the trap that it had set.

He shuddered a little, and the *ssk, ssk, ssk, ssk* of skis over snow made a monotonous music that whispered danger. Left ski forward, push with knee and back and shoulder, glide. Right foot forward, push and glide. Push and glide, push and glide, on and on and on—toward the miles of cruel climbing to the summit, toward the vast slopes of the downward run. His breath trailed in the silent air as if it did not want to leave his body. When he breathed through his mouth, teeth and gums winced at the icy bite of frost; if he breathed through his nose, the little hairs froze and cheekbones ached. His head down, his feet heavy, he trudged on while the skis hissed their song to him. *Just starting,* they sang, *miles to go. Just starting, miles to go—*

He flung up his head suddenly, surprised to find that the shocking air now felt strangely good as he breathed it in. Pushing that had been work became the smooth rhythmic gliding, the effortless moving that Lars had taught him. Gordon glanced across at Molly. She nodded back to him without words, and he knew that she too was experiencing the skier's most rewarding moment, when the blood warms and clumsiness and strain go from bone and muscle.

"Fun!" she exclaimed a little later, loosening her muffler without breaking pace.

"Fun!" he responded and increased his speed, watching her to see if she kept up.

Seemingly without effort, she glided beside him, and the snow grumbled in baby thunder from the cold, but the crust did not sink under them even with the slightest give. He turned his skis and headed more to the south.

"The cattle trail?" Molly asked.

"Shorter. Quickest way to the summit."

She nodded, and Gordon was glad she did not say what they both knew: that the trail used in the fall to drive cattle over the summit was a much steeper climb than the road. But it would cut distance from the miles of upgrade, save them hours of the way to the white lightning of the slopes beyond the summit.

The land and the snow tilted beneath their skis. They had reached the upward slopes. When their skis began to backslip, Gordon stopped to wax the running surfaces with the special dope that Lars had given them. With it they could climb without the clumsy strips of sacking that mountain skiers wound in a figure-eight about each ski before attempting a long ascent. Gordon pulled his father's gold watch from a pocket to check the time.

"Three-thirty," he told Molly, and she nodded and smiled, keeping her lips closed against the cold.

The climb began. Up and up through the pines wound the cattle trail, a thin open thread of white between tall black tree trunks. Nine feet of snow covered the underbrush here, and the pines, heavy-shrouded in white, drooped their branches over the trail. Like marching soldiers, the giant trees seemed to move downward to meet the skiers, seemed to open a lane for passing and to close ranks behind. The snow was softer here where the sun had not reached to form a crust, and Molly floundered and puffed until Gordon stopped beside a boulder that loomed at one side of the trail, pushed the snow from it with a mittened hand, and motioned to her to sit down and rest. But when the sweat on his body turned icy, he knew that they must climb again.

"Don't dare stop long in this cold," he said. "Can you go on?"

She nodded, pushing herself gamely up on her skis.

"Get behind me. Follow in my tracks. Easier for you," he told her, feeling sorry for his plucky sister. He was beginning to tire himself, and he knew that she did not have his boy strength to back her courage and eager spirit.

Up and up they climbed. The skis made a varied music, changing on soft snows or hard. Marching trees and marching skis and the watching stars wheeled off the hours in a silent world of white and shadow. The way grew easier as the trail climbed into the open to cross a naked shoulder of the mountain over crust, but the snows, iced or soft, led always up and up. When Gordon noticed that Molly dropped far behind and he stopped to wait for her, his heart was pounding in the scanty air of the heights, and his legs and arms felt as if they were made of water.

"Must be getting close to the summit," he told her when she caught up. "Feels like a lot of altitude."

Molly did not answer; she needed all her breath. He let her rest until the cold began to penetrate heavy clothing and then pushed on, going more slowly for her sake. Gray dawn light blotted out the stars as they fought up the trail.

There's no end, there's no end, there's no end, Gordon was saying over and over to himself, keeping time to pole and thrust, when suddenly he became aware that the rhythm of his lagging skis had increased slightly. The points no longer sloped up! The trail was leveling off between slablike boulders, and the trees were few and stunted by winds.

"The summit," he told Molly and felt like echoing her sigh of relief.

He led on until they had trudged across the parklike acre of flat that formed the mountain top. At the edge of the downslope, Molly flung herself into the snow in the shelter of a boulder as if she could go no farther, and in the cold pearly light he saw that her face was pinched with weariness. Her eyelashes and one lock of blond hair that was pushed out from her cap were all whitened with frost from her breath. He let her rest a few minutes before he asked, "Are you all right, Molly?"

Although her face still looked flushed and queer to him, she smiled. "Sure. Now that the climbing's over."

"That's the worst of it, all right."

"The down will be just fun. Let's go fast, Gordy."

"Don't worry," he responded grimly. "We'll go fast enough—even for you."

He eased off his pack, pulled out the hatchet, and began chopping twigs and branches from a nearby pine tree.

"Are you going to build a fire?" Molly asked. "What for?"

"For second breakfast. You look as if you need food. Did you eat much at the house?"

Molly giggled. "I guess I was too excited about coming with you and—and Mother giving in that way and—oh, everything."

"I thought so. That's why you're so tired—trying to climb on an empty stomach. Well, we'll eat now."

He built his fire in the hollow of a tree stump that was thrust just above the snow, igniting the twigs from his lit candle stub, piling on the larger branches until a small circle of heat began to drive off the dawn cold.

"Take off your skis, Molly," Gordon suggested. "It will rest you."

"But we'll flounder in all this deep snow." Molly laughed. "We'll be down and the fire will be up."

"No, it won't," he told her. "Unlace one bootbinder and take off one ski while you stand on the other. I'll do the same." With the two freed skis he made a floor on which to stand, adding to its width when the skis were removed from the other feet. "Now," he said, "you're up out of the snow and close to the fire."

"I call that mighty smart, Gordy," she said, beginning to look more like the Molly he knew. "Where did you learn all this—the skis for a floor, a fire in a stump?"

"Anybody can learn to use the old head," Gordon muttered, but he was pleased with her praise just the same. He pulled the pan of soup from his pack and tossed it to her. "Here. Heat up the soup. We need something hot and you ought to be moving a bit to keep warm."

Standing on the skis near the fire, they ate the soup and toasted the bread and meat that had been frozen in the pack moments after it was removed from the warmth of Gordon's body. Refreshed by the hot food, they stood on Molly's skis while they held his to the warmth of the fire and doped the running surfaces with the downhill wax that Lars had given them. Then her skis had their turn. While the running surfaces hardened on the snow, they sat companionably on the four skis close to the dying fire.

The sun touched the mountain summit with pale golden light, but there was little warmth in the early rays. There was no sound on the mountain top in the sunrise quiet, for the morning wind had not risen to stir the heavy-laden branches of the pines. No animal or bird lived at this frozen height.

"It's as if silence was the king," Molly said dreamily, "and the snow his white queen."

Gordon did not respond to this bit of girl romancing. Reluctantly he watched the fire die down to red coals and the sun's light grow stronger. Dread of accident to either one of them on the swift downward dropping flight that awaited them was growing larger in his mind.

"Time to go, Molly," he said, standing up. But he thought: I'd better go before thinking about danger makes me not want to start.

They laced themselves into their binders, fastened ankle and heel straps to their skis, and glided toward the rim.

"Look!" Gordon said, startled. "Tracks! Web tracks!"

The slanting rays of the sun revealed snowshoe prints that they had not noticed in the dim dawn light, although the tracks were only rods to the left of the path they had followed across the mountaintop.

"Gordy, it's that Sater and Hickson," Molly exclaimed, dismay and alarm blotting the cheerfulness from her face. "Ahead of us too."

"Couldn't be anybody else," Gordon said grimly. "They must have decided not to wait for a report on their samples. Hickson wanted to get out of the mountains, and I suppose they're going back to the city this way. Filing on our claim as they go out. Lars and I never thought of that."

"But why didn't we see their tracks on the way up? We would have hurried more."

"I suppose they followed the road. We took the cattle trail."

Gordon examined the tracks, following them to the rim of the slope. Just over the edge he found the blackened embers of a fire in a stump and took off a mitten to feel the ashes.

"Still warm," he told Molly. "They can't be far ahead."

"Then we've got to catch up with them," she said.

She stood poised for an instant to study the road, covered deep in snow and showing only a slight depression. In great circular turns the snowshoe tracks wound down the first drop over an almost treeless terrain. She pushed over, and her skis began kicking up a little cloud of powder snow as her speed increased. Gordon watched, still hesitating, worrying about his sister. But she knew the way as well as he, for they had ridden over it in the summer, and driven cattle over it in the fall. He watched her sturdy figure darting down, traversing and turning in the way Lars had taught them, her red knit cap and muffler seeming to float over the cold white of the snows. Already she was far down the slope, riding it easily, following the curves of the road when she could have cut across the turns.

Good girl, Gordon thought. She's taking time to get the feel of fast skis after all that slow climbing. He felt the muscles of his throat tighten with his dread as he looked at the snows that seemed to pitch and billow down without end. He did not want to shove off, but he remembered what Lars had once told him: "Have the scare if you will. But you must not let the scare be stopping you."

Gordon pushed mightily with his poles, and he was over

the brink and flying on the down way. At first his muscles and knees seemed stubbornly stiff, and he barely missed a lone pine that marked the first turn in the buried road. Slowly he relaxed and tension eased from shoulders and knees. The crust here on the open slope was firm and hard, with a skiff of powder frost on it that made smooth riding.

This is easy, he thought. If only all the way were like this, we'd soon pass the snowshoers.

But the headwall would be coming up soon and then a long slow stretch where the road ran through forest before it made a steep drop through rock and boulders and brush. The snowshoers might be able to take a short cut through that rough area, but he and Molly would have to follow the road or chance breaking a ski. Gordon groaned to himself when he remembered the miles and miles of flat that would follow: three miles to Finnish Matt's cabin, fourteen to the settlement of Ketchum. There would be ups and downs of course, but it would be flat just the same and work for skis.

And even after we reach Ketchum, he told himself, there are more miles to Hailey and the assayer's office. If I could hire a horse in the first town, ride it to the second, beat Sater and Hickson— If only they don't get the same idea—

He decided not to think about all the *ifs*. He would ski this easy part as fast as he could and hope to pass his competitors on the way down. On one of the traverses he glanced ahead, but there was no glimpse of the snowshoers, only their long winding track, following the road down the mountainside. But he saw Molly cut from its curves suddenly to head straight down the slope.

That's all right, he thought. This isn't too steep. I'll run it that way too.

He swung down the hill, following Molly's faint tracks on the crust. He felt his speed build and build as he roared downward toward the great curl of snow that he knew marked the beginning of the headwall. Snows, wind-driven, had swept down the slope to build that curling rim. Fear came suddenly to ride with him, but not fear for his own safety. Ahead of him Molly was flying fast. Suppose she couldn't stop when she reached that overhang of snow? What if she hurtled over and fell on some cruel rock below?

"Stop, Molly," he shouted. "Stop!"

But the wind of his speed only carried the words away behind him. Ahead of him Molly's red cap was a blur of bright color. Tossing up an arm in signal, she flung herself violently sideways into a tumble of drifted snow just before the curve of the overhang began. He landed beside her, and she smiled at him and wiped the snow from her eyes as if she had been in no danger.

Not wanting her to know how alarmed he had been, he looked at his watch. "Five minutes," he said. "I bet it took Sater and Hickson an hour or more to duck-paddle down the switchbacks in the road."

"Fun, wasn't it?" Molly exclaimed. "I wish I could always fly down and down. It makes me feel just like one of those big eagles that swoop and drift high above our valley."

"I wish we were eagles," Gordon sighed. "Then we could fly above this next stretch without touching ski to snow. You've got to take it easy down this headwall, Molly. And stick to the road. It's the dangerous part. Summertimes, when we drive this with a wagon, here's where we set the brakes—or tie a log on behind to slow the wheels. Remember? The road just drops down over this edge into nothing."

"The faster we go, the better I like it," Molly said. "Fast is fun."

The sun peered through the ridges to shine brightly on glittering snows, and Gordon took from his pack snow-blinders that were wafer-thin cards of wood with slits just big enough to see through, but too tiny to let in much snow glare.

"Put yours on, Molly," he ordered. "Wouldn't do to go snow-blind."

He climbed to the edge of the snow curl and looked with a shudder at the steep drop.

"I guess riding it is the only way to get down," he told her, adding hopefully, "I suppose we could side-step this first bad part."

Molly only laughed and shook her head, and Gordon wished that he had his sister's daring, her love of speed. He looked down to cover a small feeling of shame at his own lack and noticed suddenly the welter of snowshoe tracks under his ski tips. At the edge of the headwall, the separate marks seemed to blend together, and just below the rim they looked like the path of a toboggan.

"Look here, Molly," he said. "Sater and Hickson must have carried a piece of canvas with them—a waxed one. And they put their snowshoes together with the canvas wrapped around them and just sat down and slid. I've heard of that stunt."

"Would they go as fast as skis?" she asked in dismay.

"Almost, if it worked. And I was figuring on catching up with them here."

"Good reason for us to ski it faster then."

"All right," Gordon agreed reluctantly. "Let's go. But I'll lead this time, and you keep behind me. I don't want you getting reckless."

They stepped over the lip of the headwall, and gravity drew them down, down, down, with cords of lightning. To Gordon the air seemed a living thing that beat against his body with whips of strength. Crouching low on his skis, he leaned against the air. The rearing headwall that he had dreaded was behind in a breath. Thrusting his right knee forward, he dropped his left knee low as he swung into a telemark turn in the softer snows on the shaded side of the ridge.

"Easy enough," Molly called to him as she followed.

Slowed, they rode up and across a ridge to ski the second drop. There were trees here to shade part of the path. Soft snows clutched at skis with devilish eagerness to throw the riders. Hard snows thrust skis forward as the two fought for balance. Gordon's thighs and knees ached, and all his muscles hurt from pitching and checking, from the struggle for control in the varied snows. Two or three times each fell, bruising on the ice crust or floundering in soft deep snow, but each time they got to their skis unhurt to begin the downward plunge again. The force of the air grew gentler as the slope flattened out into a broad basin rimmed with trees on the down side. They coasted across the basin and stopped to rest where the road entered the trees.

Gordon knew that the road wound now for a few miles through a forest, taking an easy way along a shoulder of the mountain to loop on its own tracks and return by a lower shelf to a spot even with the snows on which they rested— but far, far below. There would be a short down pitch first, but there would be long and tiring trudging over almost flat stretches. He studied the snowshoe tracks left by his enemies, idly at first and then with growing concern. Sater and Hickson had not followed the road! Gordon pushed himself up on his skis and glided to the shoulder's edge.

"Come here, Molly," he called in excitement. "See where those two went."

When she came, moving a bit wearily, he pointed. Straight down the mountainside to the road far below the tracks led. The steep hillside that lay between the loops of the road had at one time been swept by a forest fire, leaving denuded and blackened skeletons of pines standing gaunt and tall. But a great snowslide had taken the trees out in a straight, narrow path to pile them in a huge heap at the foot of the steep pitch, where twisted branches and broken trunks and boulders marked the end of the snowslide's path with a huge mound.

Molly gasped. "Can we do it? Those big trees come in close and thick on both sides."

"I know. No room to traverse. We'd have to ride straight down the path of the slide. And what's worse, we'd have to stop before we hit that mound."

Molly's head came up, and her eyes danced, gleaming blue through the slits in her snow-blinders. "Why not just ram into the mound and let it stop us? It's covered with snow, and snow's soft."

"Snow's soft all right, but under it there might be broken branches splintered into sharp points. Maybe boulders. No, we'd have to stop before we hit the mound, and there isn't room for a turn or a telemark without ramming into the trees at the side. All we could do would be to fall sideways."

"It's a chance," she said. "Dare you to take it."

"Only fools take dares," he countered.

He thought then of what Lars had said, "When come time to take chance, then take—if much depend." Much depended now, Gordon told himself. With Sater and Hickson ahead in the race to file the claim, he and Molly must take this chance. He studied the down path, calculating a place to stop safely.

"All right, we'll ski it, Molly," Gordon said. "I'll go first. You wait until I'm down and out of the way before you start. Well, here we go."

Down, down, down he fled, his speed building second by swift second. He had only time to think: *Too fast, too fast, too fast.* Then the mound loomed in front of him. With all the force of his speed he flung himself into the snow at the side, thinking in the second of his fall that he would surely skid on the crust and ram into the cruel trunks and branches under the mounded snow. But hip and shoulder broke through the crust, thin here in the partial shade, and his body drove deep into the snow.

He looked back to see Molly poised on the rim ready to push off. He'd have to get out of this hole he had made before she came down. He tried to get his weight up on his skis, floundering deeper in his struggles. Frantically he raised his legs high into the air and beat down the crust at the edge of his pit, and he managed to get to his feet and pull aside just in time to see Molly flash over the hill and come flying down—fast, too fast.

"Molly!" he shouted. "Here!"

He pointed with his pole to the pit in the soft snow. She came winging down, saw the pit, and aimed for it with her shoulder. She floundered, rolling over once. The hole was bigger now, full of skis and poles and Molly. Laughing in relief at her reddened face and snow-covered self, he helped his sister out, but he stopped laughing when he saw a trickle of blood that ran from a long scratch on her cheek.

"You cut your face on the crust when you rolled," he told her. "Here, hold some snow to it until it stops bleeding."

Brave Molly looked a little ill when she saw the bright red on the snow-covered mitten that she held to her cheek.

"Is it a deep cut, Gordy?" she asked tremulously. "Will it leave a scar?"

"Just like a girl—always worrying about how she's going to look," he said, speaking a bit crossly because he was glad her hurt was no worse. She looked so crestfallen that he added quickly, "It's only a scratch. Not bleeding much now."

She laughed shakily. "Never thought I'd be so glad to fall—skiing," she remarked. "I guess maybe that was a pretty big chance to take. We shouldn't have done it."

"We're here, aren't we? And no sprained ankle, no broken legs, no coyotes or wolves slinking around. Just one little scratch. What's the matter with you? We have to take chances—some."

He wondered then at the reversal of their moods. Molly usually laughed when she had won after a dangerous risk. Now here she was, acting frightened, looking back over the way they had come with doubt of their wisdom. And here was he, who usually shook for minutes after any peril was over, feeling now nothing but triumph because they had taken a foolish chance and come through safely.

She did not respond to his sally, but washed the diminishing blood from her face with more snow and tied her handkerchief over the cut.

"You look as if you had a toothache," he teased, laughing at her, but worried because she seemed so shaky and tired, so unlike herself. This was a long hard trip for a girl, he thought. Sympathetic now, he asked, "Are you all right? If you are, we'd better push on."

Molly remained silent as they trudged through a small strip of the burned over forest to reach the road. Gordon looked back, aware with pride that they had come as far in a few mad minutes as they could have made by following the loops for an hour. Ahead, the trail now dropped rapidly in twists and turns through brush and boulders in a descent that was truly dangerous. There would be no short cut here.

"Take it easy through those rocks, Molly," he ordered. "You're tired and maybe a little upset because you were hurt and bled a little. You go first. I'll come behind so that if anything happens to you, I'll be right there to help."

Her face reddened against the white of her bandage, and her small square chin thrust up into air. "I'll ski it all right. I won't hold you back again."

Piqued, she pushed off and began taking the turns through the boulders too rapidly for safety. Soon she was out of sight. Gordon followed as closely as he could.

Let her set the pace, he thought. The dangerous part was almost over. Another mile and they would be through the rocks and out on a long open hillside that sloped gently to the valley floor. The morning sun was warming the snow now, but the crust would hold at least until they could reach Finnish Matt's cabin.

Gordon skied faster, skillfully taking the curves through snow soft or hard. They had come over such tricky places that even these twists seemed so easy that he grew careless and was caught off balance when the trail came suddenly out into the open and dipped sharply in an icy sheet toward the last of the looming crags. His skis plunged downward on the crust. Leaning into a crouch, he fought to get his skis under him, conquered, and then felt their rushing speed as he swooped toward the crag. He realized suddenly that Molly was still out of sight. Alarmed, he swept around the boulder, speed carrying him past, but not before he had seen his sister, down in the snow, just beyond the crag. One ski was twisted under her, and she was making no effort to get herself untangled.

XIII

*G*ordon stopped himself as soon as he could. *She can't be hurt! Not really hurt! Not Molly!* he kept saying over and over to himself, but as he climbed back toward her, his mind told him that he would find an injury, or his sister would not be lying there in pitiful and helpless tumble.

"Molly," he called. "Molly!"

She moved as he came nearer, and he was aware of vast relief that gave way to a sick dismay when he saw that her usually rosy face was white with pain.

"It's my ankle, Gordy," she said, looking up at him as if she had faith that he could fix everything now that he was with her. "I fell and rolled, and my ankle was under me. I—I couldn't move it for hurt. Take off my ski, Gordy."

"I'll have to lift you. No, wait. I'll dig snow out from under you. Just hold still."

Down on his knees beside her he dug until he could reach the bindings and unlace the boot from its housing. She whimpered a little as he worked the injured ankle free and lifted her to a sitting position, but she did not cry.

She smiled instead, rather shakily. "It feels better already, Gordy. Is—is it bad?"

He moved the ankle gently back and forth, probing the bones with his fingertips, and although she winced, she did not cry out sharply. "It isn't broken. Just a sprain, I think. Let's see if you can stand."

She did cry out in pain this time, after he had lifted her in his arms and she tried to put her weight on the injured foot. He lowered her carefully into the snow again.

"Does that mean I can't go on with you?"

He nodded. "You can't ski on that ankle."

"Then those two crooks will get to town and file on your claim before you do."

"I guess so." Gordon paused in astonishment. "That's funny. I—I forgot all about them for a few minutes."

"Because I was silly enough to get hurt? Oh, Gordy. And now you'll lose the claim, and it'll be all my fault. I was going too fast—just because I was mad at what you said. That's why I fell. I'm to blame."

All through her pain there had been no tears, but now they came, and she brushed them angrily away with her mittened hand, leaving a dirty smear on one cheek. With the bandage slipped off and the red streak of the cut showing on her other cheek, she looked so woebegone that Gordon put aside his own distress over the knowledge that he must lose the claim.

"Never mind, Molly. You have to expect accidents when you ski terrain like this. That's why Lars wouldn't let me come alone. It could have happened to anyone. And don't worry about the claim, because we haven't lost it for sure yet. We'll get you fixed up on a ski toboggan and haul you to Finnish Matt's. Maybe I can go on from there alone."

With a leather thong from the pack he lashed her skis together and joined her two poles with wire. "Now," he said, lifting her on, "hang on and I'll pull you. Going down this hill, though, I think we'll have to cut down a small tree and drag it for a brake."

Molly had been silent, evidently thinking hard, and now she asked abruptly, "How far is it to Finnish Matt's?"

"Two or three miles of down, pretty steep. Then three miles of flat."

"Pulling me, that flat's going to take you a long time, and you can never catch up with those crooks."

"Maybe not, but I can try." He took the ax from the pack and looked around for a tree the right size.

Molly's chin set in stubborn lines. "Put the ax back, Gordy. I know what we can do. There's that big boulder I was trying to go around when I fell, and see—the snow's all melted off there on the south side. And there's a little cave sort of place that would be warm in the sun all day."

"You mean—just leave you here all alone and go on? Send Matt back for you? No, I couldn't do that."

"Why not? Matt would bring his toboggan for me. He's a nice old man, even if he can't talk much English. He used to give me horehound candy every time we drove by his place with Father. He'll come for me. And you could go on—not lose time pulling me."

Gordon's love for his sister vetoed the plan, but his reason told him it was feasible. In the thin air of the high altitudes the sunshine was always warm, and there was no threatening cloud in the sky. If the wind came up, she would be protected in her cave. Of course, Lars had said they were not to separate, and yet—surely here was another of those chances they must take, one on which much depended. Rapidly then Gordon calculated the matter of time, pulling out his watch to note that it was now eight-fifteen. With fast skiing he could reach Matt's cabin in less than an hour. Give Matt two hours, perhaps a little more, to snowshoe across the flat and up the hill and three hours for the return with a loaded toboggan, and the old trapper would have Molly safely in his cabin long before the evening cold could set in. It was a good plan unless—

"Suppose Matt isn't home—off somewhere running his trapline?" Gordon asked, voicing the one doubt in his mind.

"Then we'll lose, and you'll have to take his toboggan and come back for me. If he's there, we'll win, because then you can beat Sater and Hickson to filing."

"Your ankle is going to get to aching worse."

"It will hurt wherever I am. Do go on, Gordy."

"All right, I'll go," he said, and then, still a little reluctant, he added, "if you're sure you won't mind."

"I'll like it. It will be an adventure."

Once he had reached a decision, he made rapid preparations. He settled Molly in the lee of the great boulder, spreading his jacket for her to sit on in the sheltered crevice under the rock. He cut dry branches from a dead tree, laid a fire within her reach, and at one side piled a stack of chopped wood.

"Light the fire if you get cold—or lonesome. Fire's good company. Here's matches and a candle stub. Either Matt or I will be back by noon. I'm sure you'll be all right, or I wouldn't go. You know that, Molly."

"Of course. Ski fast, Gordy, and catch up. And don't worry about me. I'm glad to rest because—well, I was getting a lot more tired that I let on." She giggled, pretending that her ankle did not hurt at all, and asked, "Will you leave me a sandwich from the pack? I'm hungry right now."

He tossed her a sandwich and then stood looking down at her as she bit into it with exaggerated relish. The words in his mind somehow said themselves aloud, "You're a plucky girl, Molly—the kind of a sister, I guess, that a fellow can be proud of."

Embarrassed by the words of praise that he was not accustomed to using with her, he dug his poles into the snow and sped off down the hill, stopping at the foot of the slope to remove his heel straps, for on the long flat his feet would need freedom. When he looked back, he could not see Molly, but he waved anyway, as a salute to her courage. Then he glided swiftly on over the snows of the flat toward Finnish Matt's cabin, hidden in a clump of dark pines down the snow-covered road.

As he neared the grove, he was relieved to see a plume of blue wood smoke rising into the morning air as proof that Matt was home. A dog barked fiercely and charged, growling, at the end of Gordon's skis as he poled into the yard, and the old trapper came to the door. Without taking time to remove his skis, Gordon told him about Molly's difficulty and enough of his own troubles so that Matt would understand the reason her brother had not brought her in.

"Could you go and get her, Matt?" Gordon asked. "I don't like leaving her there alone for long."

Matt did not answer, only stared with squinting, near-sighted eyes, his jaws working regularly under the scrubby white beard that was stained with tobacco juice. On his shoulder rode a huge, shaggy cat that kept batting playfully at the gentle hand that stroked it.

Impatient to be off, Gordon prodded. "Will you go, Matt? Will you take care of Molly for me until I get back?"

"I get 'um," Matt promised then. "Purry quick."

Satisfied with the answer because he knew that "purry quick" meant "right away" in the old man's talk, Gordon shoved off, the dog following for a way to growl and nip at the ends of speeding skis. Perturbed by the time he had lost, Gordon swung into a swift running pace, poles and skis working together in rhythmic movement, and soon he was again following the shallow tracks left by the snowshoers. The imprints were so evenly spaced and steady that Gordon tried to console himself by remembering what Lars had once said about the comparative speeds of skier and snowshoer.

"Old timers who snowshoe," Lars had remarked, "always claim they can beat man on ski when the way go up a little, down a little, and on flat for long distance. That is maybe true for ordinary skier which just walk on ski. But good skier who know how—any time he can beat snowshoer."

"Why?" Gordon had asked.

"Because snowshoer work hard all the time. Skier rest every time he take long glide forward. So, he stay fresh longer, make more time. On a long trip snowshoer average two and a half mile in hour. Skier get three miles—five or more if he go fast."

If what Lars had said was true, Gordon thought, then why hadn't he and Molly caught up with the two men long before this? Of course, he had stopped often to rest for Molly's sake. And after her accident he had lost a lot of time in taking care of her and explaining to Matt. It was no wonder that Sater and Hickson were not in sight, even on this more or less level land where he should be able to see them. But perhaps they were down in some hollow or behind a rise; this valley, flat as it had looked from above, rolled up and down some. Wherever they were, he told himself, he had to catch up with them, pass them somewhere in these fourteen miles. Fourteen miles to the first town! But he'd rent a horse there and ride that last twelve miles to the assayer's office in Hailey. Of course, Sater and Hickson would be smart enough to have the same idea, and so he would have to reach Ketchum first, get a head start on them. He began pushing himself to increase speed, for he found that there was a slight, steady downward drop to the terrain so that it was easy to keep his skis moving swiftly. At the top of one of the small hills he stopped to eat hastily the lone sandwich in his pack and, glancing ahead, saw two tiny black dots moving slowly across the snow far down the valley.

"There they are," Gordon muttered. "Better ski fast and catch them while this crust holds."

He chuckled then, remembering that he had a trick to use against soft snow, a wax that Lars had put in the pack, explaining its use. Catch up now, Gordon told himself, and pass them when the snow gets sticky from sun. He shoved off the crest of the hill, double-poling to get all the speed the short drop could give. On the flat again, he worked so hard that he found himself growing weary.

"This won't do," he said, talking to himself. "Steady skiing is what I need. Better save pushing for when I try to pass."

Steadily during the next hour he gained until he could see the snowshoers distinctly, moving with an easy duck paddle across the snows. The taller one—that would be Hickson—glanced over his shoulder; then both of them stopped to look back at the skier pushing nearer. Gordon saw Sater take something from his pack, hold it up to his eyes, and turn to make a remark to Hickson. Some sort of spyglass, Gordon told himself. The two changed from duck paddle to a running shuffle that took them more swiftly down the valley.

That does it, Gordon thought. They know I'm back here now. Know who it is too, or they wouldn't speed up.

Increasing the strong thrust of shoulder to pole, he lengthened the glide of his skis in an increased effort to overtake the men. Over the snows he sped, keeping always to the rhythmic motion that he knew would conserve strength and give him a more certain chance of winning in the end. He was gaining rapidly now, coming near enough to see the color of Hickson's scarf, and he was amused when the tall snowshoer angrily yanked off the red muffler and tied it around his waist. The faster pace that Hickson was trying to maintain was making him feel the heat of the noonday sun.

Gordon glanced up at the sky, realizing with dismay that he, too, was growing warm and that under his skis the snow was softening until each stroke seemed to carry him less far and yet require more effort. He knew that it was time now to stop long enough to wax his skis for the sticky snow, but he was so near the men—within shouting distance—that he hated to give them the chance to forge ahead. A few more minutes and he could pass them. And yet the rewaxing job was growing more necessary with each stroke; without stopping he might not only lose what he had gained, but drop even farther behind.

He could see that Sater and Hickson also were having trouble, their webs sinking deep into the snow, sometimes breaking through the crust and having to be lifted out before another step could be taken. Gordon chuckled as he realized that he need not fear loss of time, for the snowshoers were now being forced to expend so much extra energy that overtaking them would be easy once his skis were running smoothly again. Standing on one ski, he removed the other and waxed it, repeating the operation with his second ski.

"Hi, kid," Wes Hickson shouted back scornfully. "Giving up? Watch us pull ahead now. We don't have to stop and put on dope. Didn't I tell you webs were better'n those silly little boards?"

They did pull ahead. But Gordon, on his skis again, was

gliding so smoothly that he felt the weariness leave his tired muscles with the new ease of his movement and knew that he would soon make up the time he had lost. A few minutes later he saw the men outlined against the sky just before they disappeared over the lip of what seemed to be a slight drop in the road. He studied the surrounding terrain.

"It's Hidden Hill!" he exclaimed in happy excitement as he remembered this long section of road that, when he had driven over it in the summer, looked level, and yet a wagon always picked up speed here going down, and horses had to work at pulling up. His father had once explained that there was something in the lay of the surrounding hills that gave an illusion of flatness to what was in reality a rather steep grade. Hidden Hill, Gordon told himself, was what he needed—a good long down that would give him speed enough to pass the snowshoers.

At the top of the grade he shoved in his poles and pushed powerfully, and down he forged in a smooth ride that grew gradually in swiftness as the snows of Hidden Hill dropped away behind flying skis.

Hickson glanced back and shouted angrily, "Look out, you young devil! You'll run us down."

Gordon swerved to avoid the snowshoers, and as he passed close beside them, he caught a glimpse of the ugly frown on Hickson's face and thought he saw Dan Sater grin and wave in what seemed a friendly way. But that surely was only imagination, Gordon thought. Anyway, he was past them, and ahead lay unbroken snows. Down the slope he sped, unable to resist calling over his shoulder, "How about skis now?"

From behind came an angry roar from Hickson in answer, but Gordon was too busy to answer as he took the long slope with growing speed. If the crust would only hold! A slight breakthrough now could trip him and send him sprawling. But the crust held, and at the bottom of the hill he looked back to see the snowshoers still slogging down Hidden Hill, the webs under the heavy men occasionally sinking through the sun-softened snow. His own lighter weight and his faster speed had carried his skis safely on top, and he was far ahead.

I'll win now, he told himself, gloating. All I have to do is to keep up a reasonable speed, a steady speed, and they'll never catch me.

As he worked on down the valley, he looked around at the hills for the first time. To the right, beneath its ice, the river ran between willows, alders, and cottonwoods, their branches naked and brown in winter sunlight. On the other side of the valley snow-covered rounded hills rose to mountains almost as rugged as the peaks of his home valley. Surely he was not far from Ketchum now, five miles, perhaps. For a time the exhilaration of passing his enemies made him forget his weariness, but soon the monotonous push and glide tired him to exhaustion. He wanted to stop for a rest, but he knew that only steady trudging would keep him ahead of the experienced snowshoers, who had the stamina of grown men.

What he needed now was the courage to keep sliding one ski in front of the other one, with legs that no longer wanted to move, with shoulders that felt wooden, threatened to refuse the next forward shove. Somehow he had to have the strength of will to keep slogging on and on.

Mountain strength, he thought suddenly. Mountain endurance. In his mind he saw the great home range, its peaks standing in lordly strength. He thought of the winds that blasted away at the crags, the blizzards that swirled and roared about the summits, but when the winds gave up and the clouds went away, the mountains still cut the sky. What was it Lars had said about them that day they had first gone to Old Tom's cabin? "The mountains have strength to give to the strong. The weak they destroy."

Well, Gordon thought with grim humor, they'd better be giving me a little strength right now because I'm getting mighty weak. Only I don't intend being destroyed. Or beaten either. I'll keep going.

The sun was halfway down the western sky when he trudged around a hill and saw the smoke rising arrow-straight from the chimneys of Ketchum, its cabins looking dwarfed under the shoulders of the great rounded mountains that rimmed the bowl-like valley. His skis chattered on road that had been broken out of snow. He was in town, but he scarcely saw the people on the street, staring curiously or waving in a friendly way.

Down the middle of the street he skied between the piled snow at the sides, with the wooden false fronts of saloons and stores peering above the snowbanks. There was a livery stable somewhere, he knew, and he had to have a horse, because twelve more miles of skiing was beyond his spent strength.

He found the livery stable and in a daze of weariness unfastened his skis, leaned them against log walls, and walked inside, his legs trembling. He was aware of the warm smell of horses, the fragrance of hay, the sharp odor of harness leather, and of a man who came out of an office, looking curious.

"Well, who are you, kid? Stranger, ain't you?" the man asked. His tone changed and he added hastily, "Here, sit down on this bench, boy. You look sort of played out."

"No," Gordon said, not daring to rest for fear he might not be able to get up again. "I want to hire a horse. I have to get to Hailey—fast. How much?"

"Where you from, boy? Got any money?"

"Yes, I have money. And I came from over the mountain—on skis."

"Lord-a-mighty! Over that mountain? On skis? Takes a strong man to do that. Kid like you couldn't—"

"I did. How much for a horse? I'll have it back tomorrow."

"Well, by dog, any youngster who can ski that mountain gets one of my horses cheap. How about a dollar, and you feed it in Hailey?"

Gordon fingered the five-dollar bill safety-pinned inside his pocket. His mother had given it to him just before he left the ranch, saying that she hoped he wouldn't have to spend much of it.

"I'll take the horse," he said. "Hurry, please. May I leave my skis here?"

"Sure. Anything you want. Say, aren't you the lad used to come through here summertimes with Big Jim Stevens?"

"He was my father."

"Well, say— A good man, Big Jim. And it looks as if his boy is cut off the same chunk."

All the time the stableman had been talking, he had been saddling the horse rapidly enough, but Gordon was fuming over what seemed to him like delay. As soon as the girth was tightened, he mounted and thrust the bill into the stableman's hand.

"Nope. Don't want that dollar now," the man said. "Not from Jim's boy. Keep your money." And when Gordon protested, the man slapped the horse on the rump to start it out the stable door.

"Thanks," Gordon called back, knowing the word was inadequate to express what he was feeling.

"Horse's name is Star," the man shouted after him. "If you run him fast, rub him down before you bed him."

As Gordon turned Star into the street, he glanced fearfully down to the end of town that was toward the mountain, and there just rounding a hill was a lone snowshoer. One of them must have given up. Which one was still in the race? Sater, probably, Gordon thought. Lars had said that Hickson was a man who would quit when the going grew hard, and certainly the trek over the mountain had been tough from start to finish. The race wasn't over yet, Gordon reminded himself, and he had no intention of losing it. Urging Star into an unwilling gallop down the street, he took the road that led toward Hailey and the claim office.

I have a head start, he thought, and it'll take that man— Sater, without much doubt—a little time to get a horse saddled and ready to go. I'll make it yet.

Star was a fast enough little mare, and after her first reluctance to go, she settled into a steady pace that covered the first few miles quickly. They went by a ranch house or two, the steep roofs clean of snow, cattle eating hay around the meadow stacks. Although the road was little more than a snowy track, broken out only wide enough for a sleigh, Gordon pushed the mare as much as he could, walking her up the hills, urging her to greater speed on the level. Noticing that the sun was getting low, he pulled out his watch to check the time. Four-thirty! But Hailey wasn't far away now.

He kept glancing back to watch for a horse and rider, but there was none, only a sleigh that had been gaining on him very gradually until now he could hear the singing jangle of bells. Another quick glance, and he could see that the man driving the two horses was Sater—the man who Lars had said would not give up easily. Odd, Gordon thought, he had rather liked Sater that day in Smiley's store. But the man was a crook and had to be beaten to the filing or the claim would be lost.

Gordon swung his legs out and down, ramming his boots into Star's side. The horse grunted and danced and then broke into a wild gallop. Gordon steadied the mare, but kept her galloping. Hailey was in sight now! A quick glance back to see that the sleigh was gaining! Gordon leaned low over Star's neck.

"Faster, Star!" he begged. "Faster! Go, Star! Win for me!"

Star responded with bursting speed. Into the familiar Hailey street they galloped, past his old school building and toward the stores. Dogs, penned in by the high snow-banks, scattered to yelp and howl alarm. A sled drew out of the way, and the man driving the horses leaned out to shake a fist at Gordon, but he kept Star pounding down the middle of the street to the claim office at its end. Throwing the reins over the mare's head, he jumped off and ran up the steps. A man was just shutting the office door behind him, stooping to lock it.

"Five o'clock," the man said. "Quitting time."

"Oh, no! Please," Gordon gasped out. "I want to file on a claim. I—I have to. Right now. I've skied all the way over the mountain to get here in time. You've got to let me."

The man grinned. "Well, all right. If you're in such an all-fired hurry. Come on in."

He opened the door, and Gordon stumbled in. A little later, he stumbled out again, the filing accomplished, the ruby silver claim his to work or sell. His and his friend's.

Dan Sater was just coming up the steps, and Gordon saw, through a fog that seemed to be coming in front of his eyes, that the mining man, strangely enough, did not look angry, was even smiling.

"I see you beat me to the claim, boy," Sater said, "and maybe I'm not too sorry. And, by gad, that was a good race! You got spunk, young Stevens."

Now what? Gordon thought in astonishment. This wasn't the way a real crook should be acting. But the fog seemed to be growing thicker, and he grabbed weakly at the porch railing as his knees buckled under him. He would have fallen ignominiously to the snowy steps if Sater had not reached out an arm in support and lowered him gently down.

"Hold hard," Sater's voice said from out of the fog. "What you need is food. Rest a minute, and then we'll go get us some."

XIV

Gordon decided that his first opinion of Dan Sater had been the right one, for the man was likable, and he was kind. Sater waited while Gordon rested until the dizziness had passed, and then, helping him into the sleigh and leading Star behind, they drove to the livery stable to leave the horses for the night, and Gordon left instructions for his horse to be given a good rubdown.

At the hotel Sater ordered a big meal, saying, "This is on me, boy. It's like I lost a bet to you when you won that race. I never thought a green kid could beat me riding on a little old pair of boards and working away with those two push sticks—and me on webs. I was raised in snow country, and I'm supposed to be pretty good on webs. But that old Swede up there in the valley certainly taught you a kind of skiing I've never seen done."

"I guess I beat you," Gordon said, "because there was a lot of downgrade on the last part of that run, even if it looks flat. I think you'd have won if it really had been level."

"Maybe. But I've a notion that you beat us by more than the lay of the land. More even than good skiing. That Wes Hickson! He gave up on me, stopped at the first ranch we came to. You didn't quit. Takes guts for a youngster to keep going like you did. Toward the last there you were skiing as if something had put new ginger in you."

Gordon did not say that it was thinking about the mountains that had given him strength and endurance; instead, he ate ravenously of thick steak, fried potatoes, and apple pie. But toward the end of the meal, his eyes kept wanting to close, although he fought off the attacking sleep until he could see Dan Sater only through a fuzzy mist.

"Come on, boy," Sater said, noticing. "We'll get you a bed and let you hit the hay. Tomorrow morning will be time enough to do business. I want that claim. Do you and the Swede mean to work it—or sell?"

"Sell," Gordon answered, trying to hide his joy.

"I'll buy."

There was something that Gordon had to settle, in spite of his weariness, before he could rest. "If—you had the money to buy," he asked, "then why—?"

"Why did I try to jump the claim?" Sater asked, looking embarrassed. "I honestly don't quite know. It was just one of those things a man does sometimes to make easy money. I'm not really a crook, always been honest in my dealings before this. But there was Wes egging me on. We hadn't been partners for long, and this was our first real deal together. I let him talk me into it. No, that's not honest. I must have wanted to try cheating methods, or I wouldn't have listened. But that was at first."

"At first? Then you—"

"Coming over that mountain, I had time to think, and I didn't like what we were doing. Told Wes so, and we quarreled—broke up our partnership. He was wanting to quit snowshoeing anyway, and he did."

"They why did you keep coming on? Why didn't you stop in Ketchum?"

Sater looked astonished. "Why, I always finish what I

begin, boy. And I wanted that claim. I figured maybe Wes would rest the night and hustle on here to make you an offer. He had the money, all right."

"Wouldn't want to sell to him," Gordon muttered sleepily.

"But you will to me. Tomorrow we'll make the deal. Tonight it looks as if both of us better just sleep."

Mechanically Gordon made his tired legs climb the stairs to the room Dan Sater took for him. Pulling off boots and jacket, Gordon tumbled into bed with his clothes on, his eyes closing even as he pulled the blankets over him.

He awoke the next morning to bright sunshine pouring through a lace-curtained window and to a thundering knock on his door. "Crawl out, Gordon," Dan Sater's voice boomed. "We have business to do."

Over a large breakfast, they talked of terms for the sale. Gordon told Sater the result of the assayer's findings.

"I knew the ore would be all right," Sater said. "I've had dealings with Old Tom before—in another place. If he said he'd made a rich strike, he had. His letter to me in September told me what he'd found and said he wanted to sell. Offered it to me for $30,000. I would have dickered him down to $20,000. Are you sure you and the Swede want to sell?"

"Yes. We don't know anything about mining. And we have no equipment."

"All right. Then I'll give you the $20,000 I'd have argued Tom into. I'll not fool you. The claim may be worth Tom's first asking. The vein seems to run deep into the hill, and the property may be valuable. But $20,000 is all I can offer. We'll fix it up at the bank so's you'll know it's all fair and square. How about it?"

Gordon hesitated, not knowing what to do and wishing that Lars were there with his quiet reasonableness, his steady ways. "Lars?" Gordon asked. "He owns half of the claim."

"We'll need his signature to the papers before much money changes hands, but there's no hurry. Not as long as I know I'm going to get the claim. Tell you what I'll do. I'll give you $500 in cash for an option, and the rest when the papers are signed. Will that do?"

The proposition sounded reasonable. Five hundred dollars! Gordon thought. That was more money than he had ever seen. His half would buy the operation for his mother, and there would even be enough left over to buy more cattle. He wondered then why he had that last thought. They were going to leave the ranch. They wouldn't want any more cattle. They'd move back to the East, and the hard mountain life would be over for his mother. And when the rest of the money came, his half would provide education for him and Molly, even college if they wanted it. The sum Dan Sater offered was more than enough for all their needs.

"I'll take it," Gordon said. "Now what do we do?"

Dan Sater took Gordon to the bank, where he signed the option for the Molly Mine and took from Sater a check for $500, cashing it at once.

The banker handed Gordon the bills, saying, "Mr. Sater here is solid. Looks as if you'd made a good deal, young Stevens."

Gordon counted the bills, feeling relieved and happy and important as he pinned them into his trouser-pocket with a safety pin. Dan Sater slapped him on the back and gave him some papers.

"Here, you take these back in with you, have Lars sign, sign them yourself, and mail them out when you can." He laughed heartily. "In the spring likely. I know how hard it is to get mail in and out of that valley in the winter.

But no matter. We can't start working the Molly Mine until summer. See you then. Maybe you can put us up a night or so at the ranch while we're getting machinery in."

Gordon said good-by to Dan Sater and then walked out into the snowy morning streets of the town, dazed at the speed with which he had become wealthy. He decided that he ought to stop at the school and talk with his teacher and then hunt up his friends, although he would not tell them about his new wealth. That information was for Molly and his mother and Lars to hear first.

"When are you coming back to school, Gordon?" his teacher asked. "It's a shame for a good student like you to be buried up there in the mountains."

She was pretty and jolly, and Gordon had liked her because she had been kind and helpful to him during the short time he had been in school. He was tempted to tell her about his luck, but the telling could wait.

"Next year, maybe," he said, his hand clenched tight over the bills in his pocket. "Here—or somewhere. Molly—that's my twin sister—can go to school next year too. Before there never was money enough for both of us, but now—" He stopped abruptly, knowing that he was on the verge of telling his news, and added hastily, "I've been keeping up some —studying math with a neighbor."

Down the street he stopped to visit with Mose Field, the storekeeper at whose home he had boarded.

"Well, whang me for a mule!" Mose exclaimed. "How'd you get here, Gordy? Heard you was in town, but I didn't believe it."

"I came over the mountains. On skis."

"Over that summit? Gol durn it, Gordy, you must be gettin' as good as them mail carriers that go back to the mines. Come on up to the house. Mary'll split a placket if she don't get to feed you again. She says cookin' is no fun since you left us."

Mary Field, fat and red-faced, bustled about her kitchen, happy because a boy was eating at her full table again. Mary, who always thought in terms of food, was famous for her cooking, and she kept loading Gordon's plate and passing him hot and puffy sourdough biscuits. He pleased her by eating a big meal, but he was eager to be off, worried about Molly.

"If she's staying at Finnish Matt's," Mary Field said, "you'd better load up your pack with all the food you can carry. Old Matt never has much on hand. You can't go there empty-handed."

"I was figuring on buying some stuff at the store to take along," Gordon explained, happy in the knowledge that now there was money with which to buy.

"No need. No need. Pantry's full. Here, give me your pack, and I'll just fill it up. Let's see—there's fresh bread and that cake I baked yesterday. And a whole roast of beef, all cooked. And I'll just put in some jelly and pickles. Gordy, if you still want to buy something for him, you take him some plug tobacco. That'll please him."

When Gordon hefted the pack after she had filled it, he was glad he didn't have to carry its load all the way over the mountain. He bought the tobacco at the store, said good-by to Mose, and retrieved his horse at the livery stable.

"Sure had this hoss lathered up some," Brick Webb, the red-headed stable owner, remarked. "You must've rode him like you was raisin' hell and settin' a chunk under it. I rubbed him down good for you. Nope, no charge. Your ma fed me a good meal once when I was over in the valley. Been lookin' for a way to even up."

Gordon rode up the valley toward the mountains in the

bright sunlight of early afternoon, not pushing the horse this time because he knew that he could never make Finnish Matt's cabin by dark and would have to spend the night in Ketchum. When he returned Star to the livery stable, the man in charge, who said his name was Rudy Braun, walked around the horse to inspect it for damage.

"Looks all right," he said. "Had to check because I could see you was goin' to ride Star pretty hard. Say, did you get to Hailey ahead of that guy that was chasin' you?"

"Yes, I did. We—we were both trying to file on the same claim."

"Thought it was something like that. I tried to hold him back much as I could—saddlin' up slow, and all. Didn't want anybody beatin' out Big Jim's son. Say, that fellow took two of my good horses and said he'd bring 'em back in couple of days. Suppose he will?"

"I'm sure he will. He's—all right." Gordon smiled as he spoke, knowing that he would have answered the question differently on the day before. "Is there a hotel in town?" he asked.

"Boarding houses. But say, if you want a place to sleep, there's a cot and blankets in my office there. Glad to have you use 'em. Good food a couple of doors down the street too."

"That sounds great. I'm sort of—tired and don't feel like hunting up a hotel," Gordon said. "And—and thanks for everything."

He woke up so early in the morning that Rudy had not come to the stable and so Gordon scribbled a note of thanks on a pad of paper he found in the office, rewaxed his skis for the fast snow of morning, adjusted the straps of his heavy pack, and poled off up the valley. As he skied, enjoying the exercise because he did not have to push fast, he kept thinking of all the kindness that had been shown him since he had left home. Mountain people, he decided, were the most generous and hospitable ones imaginable. Finnish Matt, who had taken care of Molly for him. Mose and Mary Field. The teacher. Even the two stable owners. And back in the valley there were Sue and Fred Curley, always quick to help, and the McCartys with their Christmas cheer. And Lars. Thought almost stopped on Lars, who had been to a bewildered and uncertain boy everything— guide, tutor, doctor, friend. Nowhere, Gordon told himself, would he ever find another friend like Lars. To go away from the valley and leave Lars? To desert the ranch and the mountains? Was he sure—? Somehow, now— No, thoughts and doubts like these had better be put out of mind.

Gordon skied on, making the fourteen miles by noon. As he glided into Finnish Matt's yard, the dog barked and rushed to meet him, not growling this time, but jumping up as if to greet a friend. Molly came rushing from the doorway, limping a little, and Matt followed her, grinning a welcome.

"Did you beat those men?" Molly asked in breathless excitement. "Did you get the claim filed? Is the Molly Mine yours? Hurry, Gordy. Tell me. Did you get it?"

"Got it. And sold it to Sater," Gordon answered, proudly pulling the roll of bills from his pocket to show her. As briefly as he could, he told her all that had happened, watching with delight while her eyes grew bigger and bluer with wonder. Telling Molly his adventures was always fun because he could be sure of interest and appreciation.

The blue of her eyes dimmed suddenly, and he knew that she was thinking sadly about having to leave the ranch and the mountains that she loved. But she smiled, her voice happy, as she said, "Now Mother can have her operation."

"Cum in, get warm," Finnish Matt urged.

"I'm all cured, Gordy," Molly explained as they went into the cabin. "My ankle is going to be good enough to ski back in another day, maybe. Matt soaked it and bandaged it up tight, and I don't hardly feel it at all now. Matt said I was more scared than hurt—at least that's what I *think* he said. Matt's a good friend. And this is Arni—he's a friend too." Molly rattled on happily while she fondled the head of the old shepherd dog, which had crowded in through the door beside her. "And here's Sigi. She's part bobcat, Matt says. And he's going to give me one of her kittens when she has some."

Gordon put his pack on the table and began to take Mary's food out of it. Old Matt's pale blue eyes glinted hungrily when he saw the roast and cake and bread, the jellies and pickles, but when Gordon handed out the tobacco, the trapper beamed his joy and uttered a jumble of Finnish words that clearly expressed satisfaction.

Gordon and Molly stayed for another day in the spotless cabin, with its hard-packed dirt floor swept smooth and clean. Matt studied Gordon's skis, poles, and bindings and compared them with his own.

"I make," the old man said, nodding his white head in approval. And when Gordon showed him the glide that Lars had taught him, Matt said, "I learn."

A little snow fell that night, but the day dawned cloudless.

"We'd better go, Molly," Gordon said, "if you think your ankle can take it. If snow comes once, it's likely to come again soon. We may be in for a spell of bad weather after all this sunshine."

Finnish Matt, Sigi perched on his shoulder, waved from the door as they skied off, and Arni ran after the skiers until he tired and went back to his master.

"Aren't they nice, all of them—Matt and Arni and Sigi?"

Molly exclaimed. And she looked surprised when Gordon answered, "I guess all mountain people are mighty nice."

Up and up they climbed, resting often for Molly's sake, following the slim tracks cut by their own skis, but traversing the steep hillsides where they had cut from the buried road to ski straight down.

"How did we ever do it?" Molly asked as she studied their downward path on the old snowslide trough.

"You do what you have to do," Gordon answered out of his new wisdom, "even if you're scared. And when you do what you're scared to do, the scare goes away."

On the ashes of their old fire on the summit, they built a new fire and sat on their skis to eat the lunch Matt had made for them, resting for a leisurely hour in the sun.

"That's long enough," Molly said at last. "My ankle feels fine, and I want to see my mountains again."

They caught their first glimpse of the home range as they glided across the summit flat and stood on the brink, ready to begin the downward flight. Serene and austere, the jagged peaks towered above the white purity of the valley snows.

Molly stopped to gaze, catching her breath at the sheer beauty of the home mountains. "How can you hate them, Gordy?" she asked softly.

"I don't hate them," he responded, surprising himself. "Not any more. They can't shut us in now in the winter. Not if we want to get out. Neither can the snow. We beat them when we learned to ski."

But he knew, even as he said the words, that he was wrong in thinking that he had conquered the peaks. The snows he could defeat; the mountains, never. They were invincible in their strength and power, and he knew with a sudden fierce finality that he did not wish to conquer them. Somehow now they were his friends, and, gazing at them, he was aware of a strange surge of power, a flow of strength into body and spirit.

"Strength from the strong," he muttered under his breath.

And then he was afraid that Molly had heard his words. "Come on," he shouted. "I'll beat you down."

He laughed aloud as he thrust himself over the edge and Molly laughed behind him as she, too, shoved off. The new powder snow on the crusted north slope sissed in twin frothy clouds as they wrote upon it with swift tracks, gleaming blue in the highland sunshine. In sheer joy of the skiing, they wove a steep chain of figure-eights, down, down, down toward the valley floor and their mountain home.

XV

S *pring came* to the valley in May. Snow still lay a foot
deep on the level meadows that stretched from the
ranch house to the road. Beyond and westward to
the mountains, the flat plain was broken by sagebrush that
struggled to nose through lingering snow. Behind the ranch
the lower slopes, already thawed clean, were clothed in pale
young grass and in hordes of the tiny, dainty flowers that
brave the earliest growing season weeks before their bigger
coarser sisters dare to thrust their tips into mountain sunshine. Wrinkles of white snow still marked the gulches,
bowls of white the depressions; but the long months of
stuffy rooms and brief days were over for another year.

Lars and Gordon had signed the required papers at once,
sending them out with Tim McCarty the first time he snowshoed to Custer to see his girl, but this time Tim had not
been able to wait for a return letter. Late in May, however,
Fred Curley hitched up his horses and drove down the
muddy canyon road and all the way around to Hailey, saying that he had some business there that could not wait.
He came back with a letter for Lars and Gordon from Dan
Sater, and in it, as he had promised, was his check for the
remainder of the price for the Molly Mine. They sent the
check to the bank in Hailey with instructions to deposit a

half in each name, although Lars still insisted that he had no need for his share. From then on talk around the big table in the Stevens kitchen was about the money and how it should be spent.

"Mother's operation comes first," Gordon said. "Just as soon as the pass is open over the mountain."

"School for you and Molly in the fall," Mother said.

Strangely enough, there was no talk of leaving the ranch, no talk of returning to the East; it was as if all of them postponed thinking of a move away from the familiar until such time as it was necessary. After all, the pass was still closed. But one night when Molly, her eyes wistful, suggested that some of the money might go to increasing the herd, Gordon, without thinking, answered, "Maybe that wouldn't be a bad idea. Build up the herd, and we build up the ranch."

June came, and with it noons of such heat that the snows on the flats and the drifts in the gullies were ripped away, and the meadow grass grew long and rank, watered by innumerable small streams of melting snow. Gordon and Molly reluctantly racked up their skis and put them away in the barn, for only the glacial pockets on the peaks and the high summits held the snow now.

Late in June the summit road was opened. Leaving Molly and Lars to do the ranch work, Gordon drove his mother out to the doctor in Hailey, for she had suffered several more slight attacks of illness, and Lars insisted that the appendix must come out. After the operation, when she was entirely safe, Gordon drove back, leaving her to recuperate with Mose and Mary Field.

"I'll fatten your ma up for you, Gordy," Mary Field had said, a glint of anticipation in her eyes as she thought of all the pies and cakes and juicy roasts that she would have an excuse to bake. "She's thin as a woodtick lookin' around for its first spring meal."

A few weeks later when Gordon drove over the mountain to bring his mother home, he had to admit that Mary Field's cooking had improved his mother's looks. Her cheeks had filled out a little and the worry lines were gone. She complained that she had found it necessary to add an inch to the waist bands of all her dresses.

"I bought material to make new dresses for me and Molly," she told him as the horses pulled up the steep mountain grade. "It's good to spend without counting pennies. I have new shirts and trousers for you, and for Molly some pretty blue gingham, and a white dimity for dress-up."

Gordon chuckled. "You'll have a hard time getting Molly out of jeans. She's been practically living on Phoebe's back while you were gone—does most of the riding up on the range to check or move the cattle. She even helped Lars and me dehorn the calves. I just can't see Molly flouncing around in white dimity."

His mother only smiled in a mysterious way. "She'll love the white dimity, and she'll wear it. You wait and see. Molly's growing up, Gordy. Almost fifteen now."

Startled, Gordon flicked the whip over lazy Bonny's back before he said, rather crossly, "I like Molly just the way she is. I don't want her to change." He thought a minute and added, "You know, Mother, I always feel a lot older than Molly."

"That's because—after we lost your father—so much responsibility for you all of a sudden—well, you had to grow up almost overnight. Molly is catching up with you now, Gordy." When he did not answer, she went on, smiling a little, "You see, Gordy, there comes a time in every girl's life when clothes begin to mean a lot to her. The boys will be coming around soon, and she'll want to look pretty, want to—"

"Boys? What boys?" he interrupted. "There's only Lou McCarty, and he's miles down the valley."

"We won't be staying here in the valley always." When he could not answer, she went on slowly, as if she were feeling her way. "I thought perhaps you would want to make our move to the East this fall—if you still feel that you'd like to leave the ranch."

Gordon was startled. It was out in the open now, this business of leaving the ranch or staying. He'd have to tell her all that he had been thinking during the months since his ski trip over the mountain. Trying to get his ideas into talking order, he drove on without answering until they had crossed the summit and reached the place where the great range, its high snowfields glinting in the sun, rose above the long gray-green plain of sagebrush. He stopped the team there and told her. The words came slowly at first, but as he talked, they piled one on top of the last one, making sense even to him.

"Look, Mother," he said, "I've been thinking and thinking—ever since I skied this mountain last winter and got over hating the peaks and the snow. Molly and I stopped right here, coming back. And I looked across the valley and saw our mountains—so strong, so sure of themselves. Somehow a little of their strength seemed to get inside of me. I think I understood then what Father meant when he used to say that here in these mountains Molly and I would 'grow strong in body and spirit.' If we had stayed in the East, maybe we never would have learned the courage that helped us to ski this mountain."

"But in the East you wouldn't have had to—"

"Oh, I know. There we wouldn't have had to ski across mountains. And I suppose we'd have needed courage there

too—a different kind. There would be troubles to face in the East too, but—well, these mountains of ours keep us well supplied with real danger, and it's the necessity to meet danger that makes courage grow. It's strength added to strength built up from experience that makes you grow. Lars said it to me once just right: 'These mountains have strength to give the strong.' Mother, I guess I—"

"Gordon Stevens, are you trying to tell me that you don't want to leave the ranch? Do you mean—?"

"Wait a minute, Mother. Let me say it all—all that I've been planning for us. I don't want to leave the ranch, or the valley, or the mountains. Molly never has wanted to. Both of us want to go to school. And when I finish high school, I want to find a college that would teach me all about how to raise cattle, how to run the ranch to make it pay. Then I want to come back and build this place of ours into the kind of security that Father dreamed about. We can increase the herd right now and never feel the loss of money, and we can hire a man to help with the haying and the cattle drive."

"But school, Gordy. School for you and Molly."

"The money makes that easy too. When we both go out to school this fall—to high school in Hailey—then—well, Lars has promised to build a cabin on our ranch creek and live there to take care of our winter work. He says he's getting too old to go traipsing through the mountains running a trapline. We can keep a ranch hand to help him, and you can find a woman to help you in the house with the work. And so you wouldn't be alone."

"Gordon Stevens, if you'd just let me get in a word or two—"

All right, here it comes, Gordon thought. She's going to start in on how dangerous it is to live here—bears and storms and sudden illness and skiing around over mountain slopes. He began thinking up his arguments and only caught snatches of what his mother was saying at first.

". . . while I was getting well . . . to see the range . . . wanted to be at home where I could look at the mountains every day . . . not sure I want to leave . . ."

What was his mother saying? Gordon began to listen, startled, delighted.

"No, I don't want to leave this valley, Gordy—ever. Not even for the winters, after Molly and you are through high school. I'd like to go with you until then, but a boy doesn't want his mother around while he's in college, although I think now that I would have the common sense not to 'saddle you with my fears,' as Lars said to me. Daily since then I've been thankful to him for showing me what I was doing to you. You see, Gordy, I've been doing a lot of thinking too, while I was ill and recovering. And I kept remembering the mountains, realizing that the daily sight of their serenity could give me the strength and courage that I need so much."

"You mean— You aren't afraid of the mountains any more, Mother?"

"Not any more."

"And you really want to stay here?"

"Yes, I want to stay. It's what you want now, what Molly always has wanted. It's what your father wanted for us all." She paused and then went on slowly, thinking out her words. "You see, Gordy, I've come to understand that it is only the—small of soul who must gasp and cringe under the fury of our mountains. The large soul must expand and grow strong until courage lifts it high above those clouds wheeling now over the summits. Your father always knew that. Molly sensed it somehow, perhaps unconsciously. We know it now."

"You put it in a lot prettier words than I can, Mother," Gordon said happily. "All I can say is—strength to the strong. There's more than that to it though. Somehow it seems right for us to stay here. We belong here. This valley, the mountains, the ranch—they make our place."

His mother smiled at him through tears. "It's settled then. The mountains will give us strength, and out of that strength we'll build our ranch."

"Golly, I can't wait to tell Molly, though I think she's guessed what was going on in my mind." Gordon flicked the whip over Camp's back. "Get along, Camp. Get along, Bonny. Down there Lars and Molly are waiting for us, and they're going to be mighty glad to hear our news."

Camp shied at the flicking whip and then settled down to a fast and steady downhill walk. Five minutes later Bonny shied, almost sending a wheel over the edge of a gully. Then she, too, settled down to getting home.

ABOUT THE AUTHOR

Helen Markley Miller is well qualified to write about the West—a subject close to her heart. She was born in Cedar Rapids, Iowa, received her B.A. from Iowa State College, and taught for several years in different prairie schools in order to get to know as much of the West as possible. Mrs. Miller has also worked on a newspaper in McCall, Idaho, where she now lives, and has written many popular and successful teenage novels.

Artist Nancy Grossman was born and brought up in New York, and studied art at Pratt Institute in Brooklyn, New York. Though only in her early twenties, she has fully embarked on a successful career—this is the fifth book for young readers she has illustrated.